D1535296

THE LOVING EYE

◆

THE LOVING EYE

◆

A NOVEL BY

WILLIAM SANSOM

REYNAL & COMPANY

NEW YORK

Library of Congress catalog card number: 57-6207

169611

PRINTED IN U.S.A.

BY AMERICAN BOOK—STRATFORD PRESS, INC., NEW YORK

For
My Wife

THE LOVING EYE

◆

ONE

◆

ONE MOMENT the window was empty, a dark square—
and the next this strange new woman was standing
against the sill.

Her appearance was as sudden as if a blind had been
snapped up.

There she stood exactly in the centre of her little theatre of sashes and sill and darkness beyond. One expected her to bow.

He backed away from his own window like a thief.

In between them a wild spring wind drove through
the trough of back-gardens, raising sudden birds of
white paper, waving the trees, whipping a storm of
movement between all the rows of quiet shut windows.
But that was outside. In, it was still.

He stood back in the room alone and breathless, still
slightly crouched, not daring to move about. So quiet
alone among the furniture! Sounds from outside echoed
in loud to accuse his secret second—a lumber cart rumbling to its cockney cry, a blackbird's sudden pipe, the
thrash of a beaten mat. His heart beat loud as a clock,
faster than the mat. He thought: Not until that cart has

called three times more, I won't move till then—when a blackbird pounded down with a taffeta swish on the window-box, raised its long tail and slowly lowered it in a long breath of arrival, then cocked its head to stare straight in at him.

He blushed. He had begun blushing before. Now the pricking flooded pink round his ears: and staring back into the blackbird's worm-crazy glare he saw how absurd this was and did what he had all this long second been impelled to do—stepped quietly forward again towards the window; but making, though that woman was a full thirty yards away across the short gardens, carefully no sound. The blackbird looked amazed, gave a gulp and flew off. He started—the little wings thrashed loud like a silk fan—and, with his body carefully turned away from the window opposite, he picked up a book. He opened it, and thus appeared to be reading as now slowly he swivelled round and let his brow-sheltered eyes reach up off the print, keeping his head carefully lowered.

She was still there. She stood in half-shadow, refusing the full light, quiet and still and pale behind the closed window, like a figure in a portrait veiled by dust. So that he could make out much, but not enough: he saw palish hair fringed across her brow, a face so white in the half-light it looked ill, and a high collar and shirt like a nurse's, though this could not be so, for it was cut with broad stripes; her face hung forward, as if she were round-shouldered—and this weak look, and the weak light, and that look of a nurse all combined in an impression of quiet illness, of long recuperative hours remembered from the past.

How still she stood! How his upward-turned eyeball strained! After a while he put the book down and lifted his head naturally—yet very ready to look away if her eyes . . . but suddenly she was gone, he was left alone with her empty window and all the other well-known windows and their back gardens. A feather duster took her place, it went bobbing round the walls like a mad little totem: her window was raised a little above his level—he could see no more than the picture rail and the higher halves of furniture; indeed, of her he had only seen the shoulders and the head.

He relaxed and leaned his arms on the sill, now as easily as ever. He spent much time here at the window. Thirty or forty small gardens backed onto each other from the two opposing rows of terrace-houses, they made a narrow stretch of trees and bushes and lawns and walls running like a long lively corridor between all the privately busy back windows. It was a small separate world of cats and trees and grass and flowers sealed off absolutely from the other outer world of streets. Those streets were mineral and greenless—how could a passer-by imagine that nature erupted so brilliantly behind the severe façades of brick and plaster? But all over London such separate hidden troughs of garden thrive and wither; no one, unless he is invited, knows them; they are more exclusive than the most exclusive club. And such is the habit of pavements and the smell of petrol, one does not even suspect their existence.

This private world of gardens was a daily speculation for Matthew Ligne. He knew every cat, every tree, every bush, every curtain within sight, and much of the lives of the nearest people. These were never quite real—they could only be an engaging fiction. One knew their habits and watched their movements; but one could never, as a reticent Londoner, know much of their fact, their names, their wishes, their past. The clerkly-looking man pruning his fig-tree might be a test pilot, might be a die-sinker: the matron with her pea-basin could be as contented as she looked, or she could be malign with cancer. Who really was the grave, square-faced man who carried his bicycle upstairs every evening, belling it to rest on a curtainless landing brown with linoleum and yellow with electric light? Who the smart young lady in her tigerskin trousers, her window so "gaily" curtained in pink-dotted muslin, who lived next door to the bicycle man—and from Ligne's point of view only a foot of brick wall apart. And all the others. . . . He would make no real effort to find out, they remained, the more comfortably, a private speculation.

A knock on the door, and Leslie Lovelace came in with the milk. "Lovely spring morning, my lord," he said, "shall I lay the snow-boots out?"

Ligne looked down at his book, pretending to be absorbed. "Morning, Leslie," he murmured.

"You know," Lovelace went on, pattering about with the things on the tray, "what the little birdie fresh from the south said as she sighted the grey cliffs of Dover one winter's day? 'Oh, to be in April now that

England's here,' she said. I used to think that had a point." He looked gloomily out at the weather.

"It's pretty blowy out," Ligne said.

"Chimneys flying off like toppers, m'lud," Leslie said, —"why don't you go out and see?" He glared at the man he called his "lord-and-master." "I'll find you dead here one morning."

Ligne pointed to his stomach. Lovelace nodded: "Ulcer my foot. And how are the pussies?"

"Monsieur Dupont's pinched a haddock from number forty-three. Nothing more. It's too windy, you get your fur in your teeth."

But Ligne found these usual exchanges difficult to pursue that morning. That girl had upset him. There was no doubt of it. "A new arrival," he breathed to himself. He was too obsessed by these windows. The little diversion forced on him by long hours of illness in this one room had become a kind of monster. Still— she had come to live directly opposite. There she would be, a mysterious half-known figure, during all the future weeks, possibly months. He would live with her. It was a major event.

The thought occurred, and he was astonished to find that it appalled him: Perhaps she was only a visitor? Or was she just looking over the room, the flat? Was she a lost figure with a house agent's prospectus in hand, wandering about empty rooms, looking at power-points, opening cupboards? But then—she had a feather duster? Was she a maid? Why such a nurse's outfit?

"And the mummies?" Lovelace sadly asked, his mournful face glumming at the windy window. He made a half-gesture with his thumb, not raising his arm, even his hand. Ligne forced himself:

"Miss Tigerpants had a late bath. She's off now, Balearic basket and poodle, espresso-bound. Mrs. Peabasin's had to go in, her pods blew so."

"And the Average Housewife?"

"Breakfast done. Washing up done. Baby done. Cup of tea had. Radio serial digested. We're just going to stew our cabbage for dinner."

Lovelace nodded. That's the way of the world, his every down-drawn feature said, and you can't expect otherwise. He had the sad eyes and the pessimist mouth of a dealer: nothing could be trusted, nothing was any good. A life of little deals—a ten-per-cent introduction to the friend of a friend who wanted a bicycle-seat, buying and selling an armchair, or half a tongs, or a bust of Kitchener—this had fixed his face in deprecation. It was as important to shake his head at the price he himself must ask as to disapprove the object that he wanted to buy. A sagged, mouse-coloured moustache increased this effect. In fact, he was a warm-willed optimist. It was as well: he was professionally an actor, and as usual out of work. This, between the fabulous deals, had kept him in occasional work of a varied kind—the night-line of an ice-cream factory, gravedigging, lighting gas-lamps.

Matthew looked over at this bar-acquaintance "man" of his. People had mostly thought him mad when he had befriended Leslie with his roof during a period of "pecuniary embarrassment" in return for a few household services while he was down with this ulcer. But he had to have some sort of attention, and surely the less professional the more bearable since they had to spend so much time together? In any case, he liked to listen in a lazy way to Leslie's gloomy benevolent burbling, it had an easy candour that taxed nobody. People had thought him mad—but anyone should see the man was thoroughly to be trusted. And liked. He liked Leslie very much. Yet now for once wished him miles away. If Lovelace approached the window and saw the girl he would stare without reticence, even poke his head out, grin and wave. The risk was appalling, Moreover, he felt discovered at a secret. But why, he asked himself, all this nervousness? It was certainly odd: and any nervous disequilibrium, what with his ulcer and incipient eczema, must be fought squarely. He pulled himself up and said:

"We've got a new arrival."

A gleam somewhere deep in Lovelace's old pewter eyes. "Two-legger?" he asked.

Ligne ignored it: "Bang opposite. Second floor. It wasn't occupied before?"

Leslie glanced over: "Furnished. But it used to have a kind of empty feeling. You could sometimes see a light back in the passage—"

"Kind of a spare room?"

"Maybe. Who's come, then?"

"A girl, a young woman."

Lovelace glinted gloomily. "Another bloody mystery woman, I suppose. Clicking on lights, clicking 'em off, drawing curtains. Why don't we go round and call on them, for God's sake? We could sing carols."

"In April? Cruel enough without—"

Just then, like a ghost forming from the shadows, the white-collared figure appeared again. Ligne drew in a quick breath and looked down. "Uncle Fosdyke's due any time," he said sharply. "Can we hear the front door from here?"

Leslie was not fooled. He looked up at the window. On most mornings they expected a call from this uncle whose Edwardian brain Ligne was picking for his re-cuperative occupation, a short historical monograph on the district.

"I see," he said and, as Ligne had expected, went straight up and pressed his nose against the window.

"Back!" Ligne snapped so fearfully that the snap was a whisper. "Back, you idiot."

Lovelace turned, eyebrows raised in two high cir-cumflexes: "Since when such becoming modesty? And" —dropping the eyebrows to a frown, seeing something was amiss, feeling his dealer's second-sight—"why have you moved your chair back?"

"Well—you can't exactly stare."

"Since when?" Lovelace said to the binoculars lying by the curtains.

"She's a new arrival. Fair's fair. We don't want to frighten her off."

"She's just a girl," Lovelace grunted. "There are hun-dreds out there in the streets. I've seen them."

"Look!"

The girl's whitish figure, so still before, had begun abruptly to move. Her arms were braced struggling with the horizontal sash. She seemed to be pushing with all her might—or was she holding on, struggling to keep by the window? . . . for suddenly she receded altogether, her arms dropping, dragged, sucked back out of sight.

Ligne was up out of his seat, grabbing at Lovelace's arm. "What was it? What happened . . . ?"

"She only stepped back."

"She was pulled back."

"Tch!"

"Didn't you see the way she moved? She was kind of whirled—"

"Maybe she lives in a wheelchair."

Ligne looked startled: "Do you think so?"

"No. But I think you might. What's the good of sitting here to rest Ulcie if you hop up like a ruddy Mexican bean at the sight of a simple two-legger?"

"Perhaps she does live in a wheelchair. You can only see half of her." Ligne looked up at the window, measuring the perspective.

"Or she's got three legs, they glide nice on three." But then he added: "Wasn't she got up like a nurse?"

"I don't know—a kind of collar. . . ."

"Maybe it's the ulcer in you calling up the profession, a kind of love-bleat?"

Ligne still stared at the window:

"Seriously, something may be up. We ought to do something."

"Do my Aunt Mabel," Lovelace said. "Why go poking your nose in? My Dad once tried to interfere at a man and his missus. Going at her with an iron saucepan, this man was. And what happens to my Dad, my old Galahad? Are you listening? Why, this woman has the saucepot out of her old man's hand before you can say J. R. and bashes my Dad for six on his poor old nut. You're not listening. I say when he wakes up he's lying stone-cold in the middle of the road holding up two lines of traffic and a copper takes him in. Thank you for nothing!"

"I wish that window didn't look so *shut!*" Ligne said. And he thought: Perhaps it's the lack of curtains. But he also thought of all the tales of people kept locked up for years in rooms, long-nailed, long-haired, starved, sent mad. But the girl had looked all right. At any rate, her hair was short. The idea occurred absurdly—forcibly cropped? He smiled at himself. He'd got sickness on the brain. The uniform of sickness and all the paraphernalia of enemas and rubber torture, and then this empty room bringing visions of iron bars, the one hard bed, the canvas straps of a mad-cell. He leaned forward against the window-pane and looked more carefully at that other window. It looked singularly lifeless. Cobwebs and dust would be invisible at this distance, but perhaps they hung there, killing light? And the lack of curtains and some kind of pale, furnitureless, distempered dusk within?

The wind seemed to have dropped, and Lovelace threw up the sash. Fresh air and the clearer view brought things back to normal. Sounds of the morning —a dog barking, a distant pneumatic drill, the cry of a tom-cat or a baby—these echoed an ordinary monotony of noon and the daily day. Now the window opposite looked just like one of two dozen set back in the well-

known wall of dungbrown brick. Perhaps the shut silence of his own room had transferred itself to the
other window? Certainly the very fact of looking
through glass deformed things—as glass always does,
as, in another way, glass mirrors make mystery. And
perhaps the wind, the racing trees and paper and birds
had troubled him? He looked up above to the roof. A
chimney cowl, higher than the rest and curiously
angled, spun steadily. Did she then know, when she
laid her head on her pillow at night, that this cowl
spun round and round on the motionless roof that
sheltered her? He found himself wanting passionately
to tell her: then he thought no, that would keep her
awake. But such cautiousness again . . . and why on
earth was he thinking these things? Once again he put
such thoughts aside, leaned forward beside his Leslie
on the sill, and tried to concentrate on the gardens
beneath.

One could see into about two gardens to either side.
With his own and those immediately opposite, this
made six clearly visible gardens; beyond—more trees,
and occasionally a bright eminence such as a garden
parasol. Ligne's own garden had been let grow wild:
he seldom went down there and when he did he liked
to observe the natural struggle that took place between
various tall weeds and creepers, between ants and
aphids and spiders and wasps. The romantic overgrowth was formalized by a blind-eyed bust of a
bearded sea-god, and several white iron chairs now
nicely weathered.

To the left of this small green wilderness, over a

secretive wall of creeper, lay a squarely paved plot
with a single line of rose bushes, leafless, each like a
bouquet standing on one tall leg. Facing these, a single
hard upright wooden garden seat, an *in memoriam*
affair. Nothing else. Occasionally a well-fleshed soberly-
dressed man and his soberly smart wife, one grey and
the other blue haired, wandered out into this neatness
and stood not knowing what to do. Sometimes they
threw a sour glance at Ligne's creeper from which seed
blew into their precious pavement cracks; or picked
out a blade of grass; or smelled for a moment a rose:
but soon, always, they went inside.

The garden to the right, where the house was empty,
was gravelled a weedy yellow, and round the walls
laurel and privet bushes stood clumped like large wet
birds, cassowaries. Flowerless colleagues of water-
works and soap-grey churches, the yellow and soot-
green leaves of these bushes covered a dark, damp
underearth where one might expect a discarded poi-
son-bottle, a severed boot. The whole place was deserted, dismal and damp.

Opposite, and two storeys beneath the window of
the new strange woman—but why strange? No more
than a nurse come to visit an empty room?—beneath
her window the garden was planted to flower wonderfully in later spring. Trellises and pergolas rambled
with roses, canes of syringa sprayed their buds high,
and beneath this tobacco spread its broad leaves; in
this arbour snapdragons grieved and tall daisies made
their moons; there was scarcely room to pass on the
little pebbly paths winding among so much trellis and

leaf and bridging branch; its owner had painted the house-plaster grey, and against this the garden looked like one of those small, overflowing gardens of a Paris suburb, it spelled Seine-et-Oise. How nice for her to look down on, Ligne stopped himself thinking.

On the right of this florescence lay the garden of Mrs. Peabasin. This lady sat on a small jut of tarmac, neither balcony nor verandah, at the top of steps balustraded with green cast-iron whorls, and under an old bluish glass canopy. In a dark blue speckled dress aproned with forget-me-nots this old lady shelled, it seemed perpetually, her peas. The garden was tall with bean-poles, and cabbages had been planted—the path was cindered and to one side lay the grey tin basin never absent from the garden of a country cottage: suddenly in a few square yards of London a cottage garden with all its broken bricks and galvanized litter, its big-stalked leaves and a grey-bunned matron in a flowered blue apron.

To the left-hand side of the new arrival, on the other side of the gay French flowering bower, there bristled the pleasuredrome of the lady they called the Average Housewife. It was divided about equally between her and her average husband. Her husband grew tomatoes and large marrows, lettuces, onions: and somehow between them, for effect, a few ravenous lupins. The rest of the small patch was sensibly crazy-paved—and on it lay littered such as a red tricycle, old rubber ducks, a headless doll, clothespegs, a damp black tennis ball. Above these battered pleasures stretched a network of clothes lines, from which on most mornings, gently breathing the soot-laden air, there hung a brilliant sud-bright wash. This forest of white truncated limbs danced daily to the drone of an open-window wireless: or listened, rapt, to an excitable sports commentary.

Thus the immediate gardens. Beyond them a miraculous tree-growth flourished—laburnums, may, lilac, even fig. To the right the houses were quite hidden in summer by an immense plane-tree; to the left a small forest of acacias feathered the opposite end of the corridor. Such, with about twenty windows and their people, with dogs, cats, birds, babies, with visiting workmen and a frieze of chimneys, was the world upon which Ligne and Leslie Lovelace looked out. Although the prospect was not one that either would necessarily have chosen, the very fact of its familiarity had invested it with importance and delight. Together now they watched the cat called Monsieur Dupont, a slender beast, black but for paws like white spats, a white imperial and a diabolic white frown, ascend a stretch of wire trellis, poise its whole weight on four paws on the top strand—and then remain impossibly standing there to watch with waving tail the big shadow of a pigeon passing.

Suddenly Lovelace nudged Ligne and nodded at a small window somewhere above the Housewife's flat. The frosted glass, and a spouting of waste-pipes, proclaimed the room within to be water-flowing: and now through the frost a pink shape approached, flowered almost into a body, receded. "There it is again," Lovelace muttered, peering hard. This bathroom and its bather was a source of deep irritation; he could never make out whether it was a man or a woman—sometimes the figure came so close to the glass that its outline almost cleared as when binoculars almost focus; but always the frost won. It was like a pink blush, edges blurred, that shadowed into being, grew livid, vanished, reappeared. Lovelace feared that one day it would turn out to be a man; but until this happened he could never be sure and remained the prisoner of this window; whenever he looked out opposite, his eye went to this window first. Ligne was not so much interested. In any case this morning his own eye kept returning to the empty room. He was lost in a glaze of query—like a man who sits and watches a soot-flaked, invisible to others, pass slowly, like the black shape of a note of music, through the air before his face.

The girl in tigerskin trousers returned from her shopping: through wideblown muslin curtains they watched her place parcels on a table, go to the mirror and pat her hair, cross the room to do something at a bureau, pick up a book, put it down to get up again. She seemed to move very quickly: absence of sound and known motive jerked her like a puppet.

The Housewife came out into the garden, her mouth jutting clothespegs like comic teeth. She took down washing, hung up some more. She was a brisk, healthy-looking woman of about twenty-five. Clear-eyed, firm-jawed, bright-cheeked, her face was innocent of all sensuality; such eyelids were never made to lower, such teeth must laugh at breakfast but never smile by lamplight; dimples and a sensible haircut merited few whistles in the street but many murmurs of approval in the launderette. She looked efficient and absolutely happy. Through the clothespegs, in a cheerful soprano, she sang of a longlost Latin love—she was "pining for the Argentine." Her hands looked red against her muscular pale arms, redder against the white washing.

Thus the morning ticked away. And after some time Lovelace yawned, belched out of politeness to cover it, and said: "Uncle Hugh doesn't seem to be coming this morning. I don't see what you want to bother with him for."

"Oh, he's a mine of information."

"And what if he did share the couch of the divine old Florrie Buggé? All he goes to bed with now's the telly."

"Oh come. . . ."

"The amount of times I've heard you trying him about the gasoliers and him pooh-poohing you with his neon strips."

It was unfortunately true. Sir Hugh was one of those energetic old men who have accepted the modern world completely. A gadget could never be new enough for him. He listened in rapture to the boom of aircraft crashing the sound barrier, his favourite walk was where yellow anti-fog lighting turned lips black and red buses khaki, his fingers that once had savoured the finest bone china now played lovingly with the latest plastic drinking devices. He was a man of action, and loved life for itself, not for its quality. Besides, one easily forgets that the more ample Victorian and Edwardian years habitually made a hero of progress—and now this Edwardian for one was too old in this worship to change; he had become fixed before the years of disillusion, and remained the most modern of moderns.

"I'll worm it out of him somehow," Ligne said.

"What's the point anyway? So they used to grow melons in Wharton Street? So the whole of Mulberry Row was a barracks for canalmen? I should worry."

"A pleasure too delicate to explain, Leslie. Look at that bellpush painted into the wall. What does it say to you?"

"It says it doesn't work."

"It doesn't bring a parlourmaid in black bombazine and a long trailing cap to you?"

"It certainly doesn't," Leslie sighed. "Anyway you're wasting your time. You're not a writer anyway."

"That doesn't matter much nowadays."

"I suppose it keeps you quiet. But shall I tell you what the real trouble is?" said Lovelace. "Seven hundred a year free of tax. Lose that and you'd lose the pip, you'd have to get moving. Seriously Matthew, I'm worried about you. . . ."

Ligne looked up and saw real concern in Lovelace's eyes. There stood this thin, paunchy fellow, with his drooping eyes and his sad moustache, his torn pullover and his old grey down-at-crutch trousers, his big feet flat from passing too much time on street corners, his rounding shoulders showing a youthful seediness urgent and pitiful—there stood this Leslie for whom he had found a beam-end employment. And he was suggesting, virtually, that there was no need of it. How nice of him, how very nice of him, Ligne thought.

But Lovelace was already deprecating what might have sounded too soft—a pretence of hardness being something of a virtue with him: "Of course, *I'm* not complaining. Nice soft billet." But he had to add: "And quite a future in it, the way you're going. . . ."

"Look!" Ligne whispered.

The girl was there again. Again the movement of upraised arms struggling with the window-sash.

This time she was certainly trying to open it—as became exactly clear when the window went up and now, for the first time, she showed the full half of herself in the watery spring sunshine.

She leaned on the sill and looked down at the gardens, at the trees to either side. She was not a nurse, she simply wore some fabrication of collar and blouse that gave such an effect. Fairish hair, brassy where the sun caught it: yet her face pale, and the eyes darkened —mascara? illness? or just brown eyes?—so that with the sun glinting on gold this still did not look a picture of morning youth at a window. There was a note of sadness, illness, captivity: or of late nights.

As any figure resting at a window, she looked very much alone. She assumed in this brief moment the isolation of hours, with the whole still house around her, and the darkness of the room behind blind with boredom. Had she appeared for only a second, duster-in-hand, the window would have exaggerated an opposite sense of activity, of a houseful of whirling brooms and flying dust, door-knocks and stairbells: as the proscenium of a theatre concentrates an intensity of life, so the live window in the dead façade.

"There," Leslie said, "she's real."

But Ligne had instinctively stepped back from the window. "She'll see you," he whispered. "Come away."

Leslie sighed: "All right, I'll look at Miss Tigerpants instead. *There's* a girl—isn't it wonderful to think there's a real woman underneath all that?"

Ligne was now afraid of Leslie being seen at all at this window. It was Ligne's window. He did not want the girl to think that Leslie lived there; or to confuse him with Leslie; or to think, perhaps, that Ligne was just a visitor in Leslie's room. Absurdities of this kind raced at him—though he knew he would never speak to her nor even meet her, that he was far too reserved ever to make any kind of overture. Besides, this was London, a difficult place in which to befriend a neighbour.

Two workmen had appeared in one of the gardens next to the girl's, The Housewife's. They stood with saws and ladders and looked up at the acacia-tree growing above. They appeared to be wood-cutters or fellers—what are known as tree surgeons. And now one of these surgeons, an open-faced tanned young man, had seen the girl at the window and instantly smiled. "Nice day," he called, and his voice echoed clearly across the gardens. "Me and my mates is going bird-nesting."

An easy and natural smile broke on the girl's lips, so sudden as to be radiant. She said nothing, only shook her head with a little shudder of laughter.

Ligne's heart thumped envy of that surgeon's green-fingered ease. How simple! Never in a hundred years

could he have been so direct. Yet she was so near! You
could hit her with a bow-and-arrow, he thought.

Then Lovelace was suddenly backing away from the
window himself, a little bubble of lip whistling under
the moustache: "My God, there *is* a woman inside.
Now we'll see." He was rubbing his hands together:
"She's taking them off," he shouted.

"Taking what off . . . ?" Ligne said.

"Miss Tigerpants. She's taking them off! I never
thought I'd live to see the day. . . ."

"We got a ladder here," shouted the surgeon to the
girl, "you better look out."

"Cor," whispered Lovelace hoarsely, "look at that."

Ligne swore: "God, man . . . haven't you ever seen a
woman . . ."

"Not this one. By heaven, she . . . she's . . . "

The surgeons had their ladder against the tree and
the talkative one was half-way up, still looking round
at the girl, now so much nearer and nodding amiably.
The man was not even bothering to flirt, he was that
much at ease! She continued to smile, looking away
pointedly up the gardens, a girl pretending disinterest
—but always, simply, easily, returning to the surgeon
now buried in buds.

" . . . she's . . . lordy-me, I'd never have believed it!"
Lovelace had left the window and was sitting down
mopping his brow. He looked really shaken.

Ligne glanced back; for a moment he was startled.
"What on earth's the matter?" he snapped.

"Matter?" Lovelace's pale eyes mourned up at him

hopelessly. "Would *you* believe *me* if I told you she'd got another pair on underneath?"

The surgeon was shouting something else to the girl, his face in buds he was offering eggs from the nests he played at finding—and this time clear across the gardens, but soft, soft came the girl's reply: "A dozen new-laid please"—when something came from behind her, she threw back her head with a little scream, and abruptly disappeared, pulled back into the room as before.

Ligne snatched up the glasses. But the window showed simply empty. Inside—a picture rail, the top of a wardrobe. No movement. He swung round on the surgeon: who looked up at the window with raised forehead for a moment, then shrugged his shoulders—as if that was the way with all women and the world—and continued his ascent.

"What did I say?" Ligne said sharply. "She's gone again!"

"—her!"

"No, not that one. The girl. Someone pulled her back. . . ."

A knock on the door. A lady with glasses and a black fringe, a flowered plastic apron over her smart grey suit, stood there.

Both men automatically straightened themselves. Lovelace pulled at his tie. It was the charlady.

"Yes, Mrs. Orme?"

"Sir Hugh Fosdyke," came a refined voice through primly rouged lips, "is here to see you, actually, Mr. Ligne. Will you sort of—see *him?*"

◆

TWO

◆

MATTHEW LIGNE was approaching forty; he was thirty-nine years old. And he was sealed at this time of his life in a lustral vacuum of a kind that most men suffer at a later age. At thirty-nine, he suffered from a surfeit of living: it was indeed a kind of surfeit that much younger people, in melancholic transport, like to think they feel; only Ligne truly felt it. Sometimes he suspected himself of the former illusion—but he was so muddled, so between worlds and ages, with too many dreams exhausted, with too many directions taken and abandoned, that all he felt was a constant nagging question: what, on this sweet earth, to do with the remaining thirty empty, pointless years ahead? Moreover, and what was worse, he saw too clearly the pointlessness of such a vacuum itself.

Of fair intelligence, good-looking, and with a private income, he had been able from an early age to live a moving and varied life. None of the usual youthful impediments, none of the lack of money or charm or enterprise had kept him waiting. He had been accepted easily into the society he wished, and into the arms of

women—not always of those he wished, but of those
who would well do—, and onto the platforms of trains
and the ladders of aircraft that had sent him travelling
—incomparable balloon of a dream—hither and thither
abroad. And he had been able to interest himself in
various pursuits that had necessarily increased his income. Trained in economics and industrial research at
an American University, he had abilities as a marketing
consultant—and this made him a mobile and inter-
mittent business man, graduating from an executive
position in an advertising agency to his own office as
consultant in a variety of ventures—putting a French
aqualung station on its feet, co-ordinating a market
for English regional cheeses, promoting a chain of
cafeterias in the City. There had been no boredom.
He had never been tied to one situation. And there
were long holidays in between. Furthermore he had the
capacity, most valuable of all, to be interested in his
interests. It was the well of this most precious ability
that had now dried up.

Ligne's looks were so good that a number of people,
either suspicious or envious of his success, disliked him
for them: this, and a certain unnatural shyness, which
he overcame with attitudes of mild cynicism—these
were his only defective endowments, and both were
usual enough not to matter. For every one person who
declined his physical attractions, there were two or
three to accept them: and the shyness, if perceived,
was engaging, or its mask otherwise an entertaining
enough mannerism. To see him out and about in St.
James's or the Park, tanned, tall, carefully dressed,

with the assured casual walk of a man of means—it
was easy to see him as a sequence of dinners and
women and balls and the wealthier pigskin sports. His
collar fitted, there was a providence about the well-
trimmed nape of his neck; he walked with an absent
interested eye that surveyed more than saw; and a
frown between full-browed eyes signified thought.
How wrong! He seldom went out to parties. His
women had numbered a few with the years, but at
present there was no one. He engaged in no sport. His
nerves kept him slim and the tanned air that suggested
a recent return from tropical sunshine was the result
of a day's London sun—he had a skin that browned
quickly. And behind that grave and impressive
thinker's frown there blazed, nowadays, an almost
blank mind.

However, he took no interest to appear what he was
not. Bowler-hatted, felt-hatted, hatless—one could
never quite type him beyond being a man broadly
provident—he was simply one of those persons, seen
casually on the street, to whom one too easily attributes
more good fortune than is probably the truth: he
poisoned the passerby with a kind of envious wish-
fulfillment.

But underneath the innocent half-lie of his appearance lay a deeper illusion. Deep under that patina of
tan and those well-fitting clothes ached a mild ab-
dominal ulcer, and on the forearm and calf a dry
eczema itched. The passing lady attracted to this hand-
home figure would not have liked to look long under his
trouser-leg, nor at his inside opened up.

So that when now Mrs. Orme, with the ambivalence of a well-to-do servant wishing to keep her station yet infer at the same time that she was superior to it, ushered in Sir Hugh Fosdyke with a light sneer—this latter gentleman might have been similarly impressed, had he not known Ligne better.

Since Lovelace had nipped upstairs to be out of the way, Sir Hugh saw only this nephew of his who was spending too much time alone, alone. Sir Hugh's concern was always with action, it distressed him to see such pointless quiescence, particularly in a nephew of whom he was very fond. This was why he allowed his brain to be picked for that fool monograph the boy was messing with. It afforded him an opportunity to try "a few diversionary tactics."

"Well, my boy, you'll be pleased to hear I've got the brainbox to work at last. It was at number fifty-three Lanniston Gardens old Florrie Buggé lived. The house they've painted pink with the purple window-sills. I can see her standing on the steps now. Used to wear a hat with a big dead dove on it. Sign of battle, we used to say." He nearly added: And what kind of Ally Sloper's good that'll do anyone in this day and age I'm blessed if *I* know. But he withheld it, it was part of his plan to acquiesce, not criticize. A brief vision of the great contralto Buggé's purple negligée came to him. How red her toes were! But this was quickly lost, he could really remember so very little.

"Well," said Ligne, "that rules out my number fifty-seven with the glass porte-cochère. It's always the same, people never live in the right houses. Good morning, uncle," he added, wondering whether the old man was lying.

The two old pin-top eyes were staring at him too eagerly. To see whether Ligne had not seen through him? Yet it was probably no more than the wish to please: his uncle was being very kind—one could truly call him an old dear without embarrassment, his trouble was much appreciated. Ligne watched him settle himself, the seventy-year-old baby-face jutting from its open-collared shirt, the old knees showing white and thick from their long grey-flannel shorts. The sleeves of his loose American leisure-jacket were rolled back over hands long-fingered, ringed, moving in their new era still with the elegance of a decade long past. A fanatic for dress reform, the old man could never look otherwise than still decorous and formal—his body was set in a way learned long ago, it could no more move with the nonchalance of these new clothes than a Hollywood actor can walk like a Roman Senator.

Ligne tried to draw the old man out on gas lanterns, shop interiors, the steam underground: without much result. But at last he got him off—they talked for some time of the Diamond Jubilee evening of 1897, and what uniforms might have walked about the streets after the parade. Ligne had noticed at the coronation of the present Queen how unusual it had been to see officers, still in their bearskins, play out the usual evening of Kensington squares—calling at houses, walking round corners, appearing at windows: it had for a couple of hours evoked a reality of the nineteenth century. However, the old man grew talkative only because he considered such uniforms unfailingly fussy: give him khaki any day. Sir Hugh remembered then an extraordinary off-duty mufti of the Guards' officers—morning coat, white ducks and brown boots for strolling Burlington Arcade. "And the arcade at Knightsbridge?" thought Ligne. But decided not. It was, the deeper he got, all so confused. Error in every small fact became absurdly easy. Had he not written romantically of the cinder-filled flat-iron, compared it with such modern devices as the electric iron—only to find electric irons already in use in Victoria's day? At times like this he thought of giving the whole thing up, recognizing the importance of the professional historian. He put his pen down. At any rate, no more to-day. He sighed and stretched: "Glass of Madeira, Uncle?"

"You haven't any Sparkup?"

Ligne shuddered. The old man noticed and collected himself. He said kindly: "I don't expect you've any shrub handy? So I'll just take a b. and s." Silly old fool, he told himself. But now, satisfied with his little concession, he instantly felt he might be allowed a frontal attack. Age had utterly destroyed the last traces of patience.

"Bamboo, Matthew," he pulled now casually out of the air, "that's the thing."

"Eh?"

"They're growing it in Scotland. Planted during the war to make a jungle area for eastern battle training. Grew well, got out of hand. Bamboo everywhere. Well, now they're marketing the stuff—furniture, shutters, knife-handles, any old thing. Swords into ploughshares, modern version, eh?"

"Yes?" said Matthew, suspicious already. The old man was being too discursive, too elderly.

"Now they've started farming the stuff in Cornwall. Not far from where your dear Mother lives." Sir Hugh saw suddenly the picture of Matthew's mother in middle age, he had been in love with her for what—thirty, forty years? But this life-long devotion had ceased as soon as the lady began gracefully to grow old. Now she sold plaster piskies in a distant fuchsia-haunted cove and he detested the sound of her name. He often wondered at this. His love was transferred to Matthew.

He leaned forward eagerly: "Now, my boy, what I was thinking is—you're a business man, you've got the know-how. Why don't you go down and put these people properly on their feet? Study the market, investigate all possibilities? Look at the way you set those French frog-men on their feet! Lord knows, we might have bamboo aircraft yet. It's a light wood."

"Now, uncle. . . . "

"I could get you an introduction, I know old . . . "

Matthew sighed. "It's very kind of you, uncle, but I do wish you'd stop making these plans for me. You're as bad as Leslie. Look at this party he's got me into to-night."

"Party?" the old man said eagerly.

"He's been on at me for weeks. House'll be full of people who don't want to see each other and to-morrow we'll all have hangovers. Between the two of you, you'll kill me."

"Party eh? Jolly good scheme."

"But *I want to be left alone*. I'm sick of parties. I've had parties. And I'm sick of bamboo. It's as bad as Siamese cats."

"No, my boy." Sir Hugh said, for it was a long time since he had been able to feel another's point of view, "I expect you'll enjoy yourself no end. Besides," he added with a sudden perspicacity, "you might meet someone. A young woman. Yes, that's precisely what you want, a woman. Yes, you might do a lot worse than—"

As one speaks a word not in mind, absently, like a scab scratched off, a nail bitten, "I have," Matthew said.

He had said it, heard himself say it, and now as if waking up, he started forward and looked straight up at the window across the gardens: "Well I'm damned," he said.

"What, you've got a new young lady, eh?"

Still wondering at himself but now quite plainly recognizing old feelings, Matthew said, "Yes. Yes, I have."

"Excellent! And she's coming to-night?"

"No."

"Why ever not? Come, where is she? Where'd you meet her?"

"I haven't."

"Bless us, you just said you had."

"It's impossible to describe."

"So you've met someone you haven't met, eh?"

Ligne smiled: "That's about it, uncle."

"You seem to have got it bad," the old man said, thinking how good this was. But then he thought: Perhaps he's gone off his napper at last, what we were all fearing?

Perturbed he rose to go. "Bamboo," he said cordially, "that's what you want to think of, boy."

Ligne turned back to the window. As through aquarium glass the spring wind still thrashed a wild movement amongst the trees, whole branches weaved like the tresses of marine weeds. Seen from inside the room, where it was so still, from among big mahogany furniture and sleeping bookshelves and deadening thick carpet, such a movement was strangely magnified. But indeed the wind blew whole newspapers sky-high, scuttled sparrows sideways into the trees, bore off sounds to nowhere and scattered the first blossom like torn letters, it somersaulted the whole spring morning in a great whirled cleaning, upturned all life with rushing fresh clear air. Is it time, then, Ligne thought, for my own small spring-cleaning? Are there forces at work, like this wind from nowhere, that must uproot everything and set us off afresh? A girl at a window? Ridiculous. Out of all proportion. Yet he was stirred? The feeling was unequivocal? An old feeling, not felt in years, but easily recognized? Yet—winds are well-known rufflers. All over the world—*mistral, föhn, levante*—they whip up headaches, migraine and the devil in people everywhere. Surely it was the wind that had whirred a special significance, like the atonal music in an alcoholic's ear, into such a sudden appearance of a stranger at a window?

He turned back to his notes. But like many another bored man disturbed, he could not return to his chosen dullness: he was pleasantly excited, and there was no denying it.

At lunch he inveighed with unusual energy against Leslie and his party. Now that he wanted to concentrate on his new private excitement, the party intruded more than ever. Lovelace noticed a new liveliness in his friend's voice. Had he been hitting the bottle with Uncle Hugh? Not with the old ulcer too? He peered with interest at Matthew's eyes, and finding nothing got caught up with a pale high cheek-bone where a patch of black bristle remained unshaved. Bugger's Grips, he thought, we're not going to have *those* now? We're not going to have our lord-and-master with fashionable fur on his cheeks? But what's up, thought Leslie. Spring fever? Not his lordship, surely, after all this time? He suddenly thought—he's got a face like a turnip, a turnip upside down. A bloody wurzel. A bloody peachey wurzel, though, damn his eyes. Ligne's good looks maddened him—because of their waste. Leslie would have laid low the town with them, a wife in every port from Baron's Court to Potter's Bar. Few people, Leslie included, like to see the best not made of good material: it offends their sense of profit. And Ligne also offended a sense of *what was right*—it was as bad as seeing a matinée idol parade the stage for three acts, alone, without a heroine.

"Easy, easy, now," Leslie said, "I don't know what's

biting you but a party you needed and a party you're going to have."

"How many did we ask in the end?"

"About twenty asked. So about thirty to forty."

"Twenty? We could put as few as twenty off."

"Nonsense, the sausages are ordered."

"Oh."

"And I don't want you moping over your old books this afternoon. I've got to fix the room right."

"I'll go up to yours."

"How's Hugh's Hugh going?"

And Ligne said: "It's all too difficult. I may give it up."

Lovelace stopped the spoon about to enter his mouth and let his jaw sag slowly open. A taper of mousey moustache drank at the yellow custard thus surprisingly offered.

"Roll me over!" he said.

And then: "I'll be out of a job at this rate," he pleaded, "think of poor Les."

But Ligne was not listening, was finishing his custard quick, lashing with his spoon like a schoolboy crazy to get down. It had suddenly occurred to him that up in Leslie's room he would be able to see clearly down into the girl's window! Why in hell hadn't he thought of this before? Then he too paused with the custard spoon in his mouth. This sly, salacious Leslie would always be in a position to look down into that room! "He'll be out of a job all right," Ligne breathed out over the custard. For almost a minute the two men alone in the dining-room faced each other with custard spoons at their mouths, jaws open, glaring mutual suspicion. Their expression, lower jaw dropped and working, was the same as that of any two tom-cats meeting in the gardens outside.

Ligne raced up the stairs two at a time, his ulcer forgotten.

Leslie's room was part of another world. The bed still unmade, at the bedside table a telling assortment —a half-drunk bottle of beer flat from the night before, half a tin of drying sardines, an evening paper folded at the racing page, a pocket-smeared copy of *Stage,* a bile-pill bottle, cigarettes stubbed out in a tin-lid (there were plenty of ashtrays in the house, but Leslie was a man who disliked throwing away anything as useful as a tin-lid). From a nail hung several frayed, striped ties; a pair of washed pants hung over two bookrests—volumes of the Home Handyman, the Antiquarian's Yearbook, and for some reason Walt Whitman beneath; and among assorted purchases of old ornaments—he was at present painting new spots on two chipped china dogs—a general assortment of tools and brushes and paint-pots and thrown-off clothes. An inveterate bedsitter, Leslie had settled in according to his lights. But about the whole heterogeny there was one consistent factor—not one single bottle of oil, medicine, paint, nor empty bag of sweets nor carton of cigarettes nor even box of matches was quite empty: always a little, even down to one match, was left in the receptacle. Leslie was a rainy-day man.

Now Ligne strode through this mess resenting its every evidence. He had always been tolerant, feeling warm towards Leslie's improvisatory nature: but now, to get at the window quickly, he grabbed with real anger at the china dogs propped on a table in the way. Fresh paint came off on his hands. He stood thus at the sill with his hands held out in a cupped attitude of despair as, at first sideways in case the girl was there, he peered anxiously down into her room.

He was astonished to see that it was only half-decorated and in great disorder. From downstairs he had imagined that the bare upper friezes ran down the whole wall like the dust-white paint of a studio or a hospital. But now he could see bright-coloured wallpapers of fashionable design in stripes and careful blodges, even different wallpapers on different walls— even that old trick. It might have been Miss Tiger-pants's den. (But there are people who follow fashion simply through expediency? Ordering what is there and disregarding it, too busy about more important things? Better to think that.)

So she was moving it! And then standing at the window, his hands outstretched where the dogs' new spots had soiled them, Ligne again reviewed his emotions. Certainly there was nothing sinister about this gay and voguish room. He thought again what he had suspected, with a kind of disappointment, all along— that she had simply been pulled back in that urgent way by the sound of a bell.

After all, people everywhere were now on the move. It was spring and the painters were out. A gusty spring —"bad weather for sandwichmen" as the saying goes, hard on their back muscles. And up on their cradles the white-suited painters swung and shuddered and flapped against smoke-brown brick, stroking their sills clean and cream and fresh. They hung out of windows, stabbing upwards; they straddled off ladders onto cornices, chipping like white schoolmasters at the brownboard; they stood upright on their ladders, legs together, like preachers praying the wall clean; and they squatted down on the pavements, white necromancers muttering as they stirred their pale and leaden brews. It was as if a race of man-sized white spiders had come out over the walls, called from nowhere by the new spring warmth.

In a weather one day bright, one day brightly dull, these spidermen laid their gleaming trails along terraces all over the town, fresh paint shining for geraniums to come: but first the wild undercoat colours freckled the streets—red lead dappled a devil's nævus on a portico, a telephone kiosk turned pale lavender, primrose yellow fired the park gates, bright ochres abounded and cones of golden sand rose from the grey pavements. The promise of warmth, the sudden dizzy coming and going of good weather brought out buds and roadmenders, the trees flared a lace of yellow sparks, tar-engines and drills dazzled the air with asphalt smoke and rattling clouds of dust. Everyone was busy, all London was putting on a new face, hope and hot sunlight and brisk new winds invigorated limbs and the air. Sometimes it seemed that the heavy sweet smells of paint and smoke must overpower the true scents of spring—but then these would come bursting through, green smells as heady as hay, sun-smells that opened the nose like a flower and pumped life and dizzy new lusts into wintershrunk lungs.

Ligne breathed at this air, looked that window at last fair and squarely in the eye—then suddenly noticed that down in her garden Mrs. Peabasin was looking up at him curiously. She stood staring unashamedly, as people may feel they can do to others with such as pigeons on their heads. Ligne saw it was his hands. He must look like Job beseeching Heaven for peace—so for Mrs. Peabasin's sake he stretched the hands further out as if he were testing for rain and looked up anxiously at the sky. It was bright blue. In the last minutes the wind had fallen, the English spring had cut one of its more engaging capers. It was like the afternoon of a faultless summer's day. Ligne drew back his hands as if the sky scalded them.

A whistling kettle piped its piercing note from a basement somewhere. He remembered he had heard others—so it must be well after four o'clock. Time to go down and get ready for this party.

"The weather should hold good," he said to himself as he turned in. Why, since the party was to be held indoors? To calm his troubled mind?

◆

THREE

◆

It was now as if the turbulence of the day had removed itself from outside to the enclosure of the sitting-room, leaving a deep and windless quiet over the
evenings gardens. The party was gathering momentum.
And still the front doorbell rang: all attempts to leave
the front door open failed—each guest imagined his
arrival to be somehow unique and closed the latch
with what he thought a good deal of consideration behind him.

The noise was great. It was the well-known drone,
like a hive excited, of thirty or forty people talking at
once. From the street it sounded like a hundred high-
pitched tape-recorders making the same point at once.
It also sounded like heat, footache, disquieting new
faces, watery little drinks, and small staccato talks that
never reached their point. The marvel was that hearing
it, no one turned silently homewards. Ligne's friends
mostly came from the half-prosperous half-world of
Knightsbridge, Chelsea, Kensington. Some came from
painted-up terrace-houses with primrose doors and a
couple of bay-trees, former artisans' dwellings that now

cost them a quarter of their upper class incomes to rent. Condemned to such cramped quarters it was little wonder they valued so much their annual liberty—they seemed to talk of little but going abroad. Others lived high in concrete-smelling flats; yet others in solid Edwardian maisonettes of red brick that smelled of french polish, lift-shafts and the porter's uniform.

Here at last convened were the faces of the backs of heads one sees reading, still as wax figures, through uncurtained windows at evenfall. The momentary persons passing without sound across rooms one would never enter. The exclusive owners of the tinkle of glasses and the ends of bookcases, of statues, lamps, chimneypieces half-hidden and privileged in a mystery of shaded yellow light. On winter afternoons their firelight flickers in warm shadow, buttered buns and Vogue-fingering teas are to be envied them. At night, they are a chink in the curtains. Excluded, a passing eye in the street, one feels almost offended.

Living question-marks, here with their hats and jewellery, their ties and their watchchains, they were paraded at last for anonymity to be broken. An exciting prospect, mutually felt. But—a moment's conversation and the bubble was burst. Each face as it moved fell into a type and anonymity was sacrificed—after a very few words people felt they knew a great deal about each other.

Trying to get to the window, buttonholed and bemused, Ligne moved among what he suddenly felt might be a travel agent's office party. Up till mid-December these people had talked of where they had been that year for their summering: from Boxing Day on they discussed the next year's plan. It was almost religious, with a properly pagan recognition of the winter solstice. One or two heretics bronzed from the snow-sports were regarded, enviously, as not quite playing the game.

"We've just come back! But Susan and Ian are leaving Monday fortnight!"

"We *were* going earlier but Kim was kept here. So now we've got July to look forward to. Harriet and Dymphna are in Cannes, and Michael's going to the Azores in June—after the flores, one can only suppose."

"Hester and I want to get away from absolutely everything."

"I know a little place on an island."

"Oh *do* tell."

"It's very, very quiet."

"But that's positively our tea! I suppose there's something to do in the evening?"

"Nothing."

"Oh."

"Taormina's finished."

"One could cross to Africa if it wasn't for the flies. They do tickle so."

"Slapless tickle no bon, eh?"

"It's to be *Shanklin,* dear. Father can't stand all that ghastly foreign money again."

"The long *midi* mornings boiling in the *bureau de change?* I don't blame him."

"Athens, Mycenas, Varna with a visa."

"Just Juan."

And just as not everybody came from the pink-washed cottages of nineteenth century artisans so they did not always speak of their annual migrations over-seas. Some of them, for instance, spoke of the food they had eaten here and there.

And others spoke of the latest, most popular murder, confessing with coy abandon that their favourite read-ing was the more sensational Sunday Press. Homosex-uality was eagerly touched on, casually stiff upper lips above the roving tongue:

"What do *you* say's his sex-life then?"

"Oh, married and queer, I suppose."

Among the older of these youngish people, paunchy men with bagging eyes and women stoutening into authoritative cylinders, like supervisors in the better-class tea-shops, the talk sometimes turned on schools. Ligne heard one man a few shoulders away appealing with guilty emphasis:

"You know, old man, I don't see why, actually, after all, when all's said and done, we shouldn't if you look at it sensibly, *have-them-done-on-the-State!*"

"I've always said so, old man."

"Glad you agree. By the way, where's Brian going?"

"Marlborough, old man."

But even more frequently the talk turned on what were called, as one word, foreign-girls.

"Pamela's Italian left in a week!"

"We had a Spaniard for twenty-four whole hours."

"It's their friends of course, they're the enemies."

"It's the luck of the throw. Claudia's got an old girl from the Saar for life. Can't bear the sight of her. Offered to pay her fare back, offered her a *plebiscite*. But oh dear no, she didn't want to let Madame down! Arthur spends half his time in the public library: they say there's a chance he'll soon be quite literate."

But nobody could altogether be blamed. To stand balancing a cigarette and a glass and a little sausage with only two hands was not an ideal condition for the weaning of good conversation. Perhaps feelings ran deeper than words, and then deepest at points of divergence. The formidable English sense of class justice was at play. Unbelievably subtle discriminations were at work beneath talkative English masks. Eyes darted at little stitches in clothes, ears detected minute modulations of accent. Behind smiles carved in the wood of good manners, these stiff and terribly sensitive people put each other through the sieve.

Sometimes the differences of appearance were simple —as with a friend of Leslie's dressed in mixed Edwardian and American clothes, his neck unwashed beneath a most expensive haircut, a velvet-collared coat sticking an inch away from his shirt-collar. This young man had lost his soul to another kind of Edwardian waistcoat, modelled with reserve by an old-established West-End tailor, worn by a friend of Ligne's. Leslie's friend felt himself superior to Ligne's friend, his own waistcoat hit the eye more; yet an awful seventh sense told him that Ligne's friend had something he had not got, and he did not know what it was, and how would he ever know, and so he felt he must go to Ligne's friend and flash his waistcoat about near the other waistcoat, to overpower it somehow, to shine and shine it away.

But a woman-friend of Ligne's, who prided herself on a chic reticence of dress, who had walked miles of pavement in search of ever more subtly drab materials, colours of exquisite dirt and most expensive—this woman had her eye on another dressed flamboyantly and felt wild to go over and nudge her rich soot against the other's sunrise. Yet she never did, she trusted so few people to appreciate the substance in her shadow: especially the men.

But as a whole, with some comparative easing of class distinction bred of wars and taxation, people did not get on together too badly, they all smiled and sought for common ground. Yet—who would have asked whom home?

Among these, then, Ligne moved with his tray of glasses, listening for the front door and trying to pass through the crowd to get to the window. But finally there he only found himself told amiably by an unknown man of middle years what a crush it was; and asked by another what was his line of work; and then,

just as he was at last about to look out he was ad-
dressed by a girl with small hurt eyes who appealed:
"Do you know many people here?"

"No," he was able to answer.

A smile of commiseration from under her lipstick
and light moustache:

"Neither do I. I often wonder why one comes when
one doesn't know a soul."

"Quite."

"After all, one needn't, need you?"

"Well, yes, really. You see, I'm the host."

This classic encounter brought its usual embarrassed
titter. But through it Ligne was able at last to steal a
glance out of the window. He saw the worst. The girl
was there, and there was a paintbrush in her hand.
There, in this lull in the gusty weather, when all the
real painters had gone home, she alone had begun her
task! To the belling sounds of glass and bottle over the
quiet gardens—there she was alone with her solitary
task . . . if only he could help! He found himself suddenly ashamed of his party—drinking and laughing
while others worked!

"You look so tanned," he heard himself asked, "I'll
bet you're just back from Spain or somewhere. . . ."

"I've never been there," he said hurriedly. That tan
he had picked up in a deckchair near the Dell. But did
that girl over there know, he wondered anxiously, how
to thin paint with turpentine?

Then the girl addressing him tossed back her glass
of gin: "Have you seen the baby?" she asked.

"Baby?" Perhaps she used turps substitute? But did she know it would crack later on?

"The baby somebody brought to the party. In its own little cot. It's too sweet."

"A baby to the party? Don't be absurd." Well, he only hoped it was a good brand of substitute turps.

"It's upstairs. *Such* a darling."

Upstairs! Of course! He fixed a broad smile on his new companion and then began pushing a way through the crowd. Fingers grasped his arm as he passed. Expertly he introduced two people who had already been introduced twice before. An enormous black cartwheel of a hat hit him in the eye. Still he plodded on, determined to get upstairs to Leslie's window.

There was now a light smell of gin in the air. Heads bobbed smokily through evaporating essences of spirits and scent. Women, who had at first looked serene compared with their men ruffled by a day at the office, were now reddening and taking on a light disorder; tosses of the head haloed them with wisped hair, sweat broke through make-up. Meanwhile, waistcoat pockets were filling with sausage sticks, trouser cuffs with cigarette ash.

Ligne at last broke through—only to find himself face to face with Leslie. A fresh tray of drinks was thrust in his hands. "Stiff ones," Leslie whispered fierce in his ear. "They've had a couple of rounds of water. This'll put some gyp into things." But then his ulcer rose to help him, the pain hit so suddenly he could only push the tray back into Leslie's hands. It often discovered its own escape route in this way. Now he had only to say: "Sorry," and clutch at himself for Leslie to understand. "Hard cheese," the mournful moustaches kindly mouthed. "Run along for a glass of bic, then."

He climbed quietly up to Leslie's room, now filled with hats and a few coats and sank happily onto a chairful by the window to watch. He kept his face half-hidden by the curtain.

He could see the girl's golden head patiently following the slow brushstrokes. She held her head to one side. He knew her tongue was out—and she seemed the younger and more precious for this. Alone and hidden, and with time to spare, he felt a sudden detachment. He saw for the first time exactly who this girl was: she was the girl seen for a moment on the street, or in a bus, in the park or in the train, anywhere that made her unattainable—and is remembered forever. Her one important quality is her passing. Her merit is anonymity. If you speak to her she vanishes, leaving someone fairly like her in her place. Either way, passing or accosted, she is unattainable.

But this one, he considered, has come here to this window which is part of my life—by a wonderful chance she cannot pass! A piece of luck indeed! And what is my impulse? To meet her, of course, to speak to her—to do in fact exactly what I know will destroy all that is valuable in her. Yet . . . my very cowardice— or reserve or what you like—will prevent this? An errand boy may smile at her—myself never? Then that's another piece of luck.

The girl paused her brush in mid-stroke and turned her face full in his direction. He shrank back. But she was only looking at the window below, where the party was. She still held her head to one side, listening. He could hear the party sound plainly—and instantly it sounded not as an unpleasant noise but as it must have echoed to her, music of enjoyment on the evening air, music from childhood when in the house below parents began their magical, grown-up evening. A melancholy joy filled him.

When suddenly a chair creaked behind in the empty room! He glanced back over his shoulder: but there was only the other coat-hung chair, the bed; no one there. Yet the same little noise, like a bleat of stressed wood, sounded again. Then rose abruptly from a creak to a belly-drawn wail, a terrible sound as dissonant as the torment of a tom in rut.

Matthew leapt to his feet. His heart thumped—there was appalling pain in the noise, it was a sound of loud and lonely soul-torn distress, something hollow and bad, and his mind went to tales of summery ghosts, of presences in the daylight—as now the room filled and filled to its furthest corners with sound . . . until his ears quickened and led him to the source, an oblong box of white plastic wedged between overcoats on the bed. And inside, among what looked in the half-light to be swathes of tissue paper, he saw something move.

He crept over and saw in the box the face of what seemed to be a small, bald, angry old gentleman. The gentleman had no teeth. His legs were caught up in some sort of loose white Indian trousers. His gum like a venomous underlip execrated the world and all in it, and an aroma of hot wet wool arose thick as the

howl itself . . . when a smart young woman came round
the door, stubbed her cigarette out and said to Ligne:
"So you've found someone very precious, have you?
Isn't he a little man?"

"He's very small," Ligne said, much relieved that
this woman had come. Alone with the baby he had felt
dark and huge as a preying eagle; he had never seen
one so young, and feelings had risen in him of intense
curiosity and dangerous power, mixed with terror at
anything so small, so raw.

"He's only six weeks," the woman said.

"He's very wonderful, Margot," Ligne said, finally
recognizing her, the wife of his new doctor.

The woman shuffled the child up and down, the
night and the howling deepened.

"It's the wind," Margot said.

Ligne looked anxiously out of the window. "It's getting up again, is it?" The weather, somehow, had become the province of that girl at her window.

"No, *his* little wind, silly." She banged the child
down on a cushion—how roughly she handled it, no
wonder it stopped crying!—and went over to switch
the light on.

"Time for his feed. You don't mind do you?" Magically, part of this Margot's dress fell open and a rich
wealth of breast poured out, white and brown, vanilla
with a coffee centre. Margot put the little old man to
this, as, in nervous access, Ligne's ulcer bit him inside.
Has it not been said that ulcers have little round teeth
of their own and that you have to feed them? Was his
then envious of the baby's good fortune?

Margot was a handsome young woman, painted and jewelled. This lent a wicked look to what otherwise was a natural enough exposure. At least, Margot believed it to be natural. She had seen it so often among peasants in Italy. But Ligne was no Latin and Margot no peasant. He who had long given up smoking wanted badly to place a cigarette to his lips. He turned away to the window—and only then remembered anxiously the girl, whom this episode had abruptly washed from his mind. Could she have seen? What would she think? His hand grabbed for the curtain. But he saw she had gone in, and only half-drew it.

Now the girl turned her light on too. For the first time her room was exposed in bright detail by the bare electric light. The room instantly took on the look of a kitchen.

He peered forward—he could not bear now to leave the window: behind him the silent suckling continued, in front of him lay the silent lighted window, and in the small of his back the awful eye watching him watch.

Fortunately Margot seemed too engrossed with the baby to notice much. She was talking hard: "O such a big little man we are, aren't we? We haven't a single trouble in the whole wide world, have we? 'cept for our wind—there, the gong's gone for Dinneford's, hasn't it?"

But she was really talking less to the baby than to cover her embarrassment with Ligne: she spoke high and fast, forcing down modesty in the interests of nature and liberty. In this Ligne was lucky, for normally there is no such relaxed observer as a woman with a child at her breast.

"And we have our bunny trouble, too—don't we now? It's this damned myxomatosis, Matthew. When they grow up there'll be no bunnies left at all. So frustrating. We've had to get all the rabbity toys out of the house—and you've no idea how many there are— and then unstitching them from all the pillowslips and his bibs and the little dresses, new wallpapers too. . . . "

"Brer Rabbit," said Ligne, as the girl came back into her distant room and sank to her knees by a pot of paint. To her *knees!* "You'll have to look out for Brer Rabbit."

"I know. And all Bea Potter. I don't know what they'll have left."

"King Arthur and—"

"That *awful* table," sighed Margot. "Now does he want to change over? Matthew, you wouldn't be an angel and get me a drink?"

"Of course." But he hesitated. What might he miss? Who else might enter that room?

"It's particularly thirsty work!" laughed Margot, easy as a cracked bell. "There's my glass on the—"she stopped herself just in time—"above the fireplace."

Ligne went down to get her drink. The party, past its full swing, was taking shape: early diners were leaving, hardened drinkers settling in. One or two people said goodbye to Ligne at the door, thanking him effusively for what must have been an unexceptional drink or two. Then a woman with a striped hat hanging down one side of her face began to congratulate him on a set of prints hanging on the wall. As people do, she chose to speak of the patch of room where she stood. It was not one Ligne had taken care about, or cared for. He wanted to take her to *his* patch. He hesitated, remembering what faced him upstairs, wondering whether to stay down a few moments. But the thought of the window drew him back against all better sense.

The baby was in a reversed position. As he handed Margot the drink, he noticed quite a lot of fine hair straggling at the baby's neck: the wobble of such a large head on so frail a neck, the lack of a haircut, the stupor of application, reminded him of an elderly don nodding at a hot day's cricket. Margot took the drink, and sitting there with her hat on, her legs apart for support, she began to look like a lady half-seas over in the four-ale. She said: "It *is* fun having babies at parties, isn't it? Think of all the mothers who used to be tied at home! But I expect you men disapprove heartily," she added, accusing, coy.

"Oh no, not at all."

"Admit it!"

"But I couldn't," Ligne's voice rose in anguish as he edged to real anguish at the window, "agree with you more." And still the girl was painting, slowly, slowly, alone in her lighted room.

"Demand feeding," asserted Margot, ignoring several thousand years of history, "is the latest thing."

If holding a glass she wore a hat then she should cross her legs, Ligne thought. "Won't you take your hat off?" he found himself asking, eyes on the girl who

had risen from the floor and was standing as always
so very much alone, so isolated in her frame, stretching.
The wet paintbrush was still in her hand. "You'll
dribble it!" Ligne yelled inside his ears.

"Don't you like it?" Margot asked. "Perhaps it would
be more comfortable off. *You* take it off for me."

Something flashed in Margot's eyes, as if both eyes
had grown bigger and in them liquid danced to drown
him—or did that raffish position, straddled and hatted,
only suggest this? He had heard that women are wild
after childbirth—even the law refused to hang them
then—was it for a year? He said quickly what is often
the best thing to say at such a time rather than invent,
he invoked a secondary truth: "But it looks so beautifully out of keeping—now you're feeding him. *Do* keep
it on!"

Margot laughed. Lip-service at least done, Ligne
could turn to the window. But lip-service is never quite
enough, she was noticing him now: "What's so inter-
esting out there?" she said. "You're quite glued."

But what that girl did then in her window made him
catch his breath. Arms stretched wide she turned the
stretching into a smooth swirl of her whole body, on
that one spot she made a pirouette right round as a
dancer might! Bright-lit within her proscenium, the
effect of artifice or acting was extraordinary . . . and in
doing it she must indeed have spilled paint, for one
arm in mid-pirouette went to her mouth in horror, a
natural gesture became in the window large mime,
and she sank to her knees nodding at the floor, and
wobbled her head from side to side as if suddenly mad,

as children make idiot motions on purpose—or indeed as young babies let their heads nearly wobble from their necks, and there was Margot repeating: "Glued, dear!" He looked quickly away from the window.

But Margot insisted, so he looked back to the gardens searching for an excuse. Nothing but a beam of light among chequered curtains, the sound of a basin's ring and the radio from the Average Housewife. Then a sudden shadow, big as a goddess, as a ginger Persian, tail high, breast swollen with pride, stepped onto lighted crazy pavement and off. Suddenly Ligne remembered the young owl that habitually sat on the television H opposite.

"There's an owl," he said, "on the aerial."

"What?"

He knew Margot could not get up. Glaring at the empty aerial thin as ship's rigging against the night sky, he said that the owl sat exactly in the centre. He could see it distinctly, he said, like an owl in a children's book.

"With The News reeling across each eyeball?" Margot said?

"Owls come in from the park," Ligne said, "they make a noise all night like someone trying to say tu-wit-tu-woo and just missing."

"Whenever I hear a pigeon," Margot said, "I imagine it staring up at the nest it's just been pushed out of saying 'that God-damned cuckoo, that God-damned cuckoo' over and over again. You know, da-da-da-*da*-da, the way they go."

Would that girl know how to get those paint-spots

up? But suddenly, still talking about the absent owl, he remembered what had quite passed from his mind in his pleasure at seeing the girl again, he remembered how she had so curiously been pulled back. Perhaps at last, now the room was lighted, he would see what happened. . . . He settled down to watch and time passed, Margot talked, the baby sucked, and the girl painted on and on and on.

How intense is the concentration, how timeless the reiteration, of such tasks seen through windows! How could she bear to continue so equably—without even a glass of water, a cigarette? Cut off from the many small shadows and lights and objects and sounds inside the room with the girl, cut off from all those small sensations that made the moments of a long task alive. Ligne could see only the task itself, in terrible monotone. And once more he had the impression of a prisoner.

"The sparrows in my garden," Margot went on, tidying the baby but distracted now by birds, "think the slenderest rose-bush a tree, the damnfools. There they go, fat things, swinging on twigs—"

"Buzzards have been known to steal babies," Ligne said with a savagery that surprised him.

He turned abruptly from the window. He refused to go on watching that girl paint. There was something insolent in her equanimity. There was always, come to that, something insolent about all people who left their curtains wide at night. Do they not realize people are looking at them? Yet there they go about their lives, without bothering, aggressively unselfconscious, bragging like half-naked bathers strutting about a beach.

"Margot, wrap that child up and come and have a drink," he snapped, suddenly efficient. "Have you seen the baby blackbirds we've got? Brown as berries these blackbirds are, bigger than their mums. They go down like ninepins to the cats."

"Don't be disgusting. We'll give him cats, won't we, my precious? Now—winksybies!"

On the way down with Margot he thought: She only left the window open for the smell of paint. And felt sorry for what he had thought, and wanted to go back somehow to make retribution with his presence.

The party had spread. Two or three people had got as far as the kitchen, with its sink full of bottles and watering ice, with its dirty glasses queued among a litter of wet ash and stubs like walking wounded. In the larger, now emptier room, knots had formed, leaving wide stale carpet-space tired between. But even thus dispersed the guests made greater noise than before, the gin had risen and they all laughed more loudly, or moved more freely, making a noise of shape with their more active bodies, arms flung and heads circling.

People were easier, and had started telling each other of all the dreadful things that had happened to them and their friends. Leslie was at it, finishing with mournful satisfaction some story of an alcoholic friend: " . . . so he was on the train and wanted another, he walked right through the corridor, stumbling through seven carriages of bags and people looking for the restaurant car, until he got to the guard's van and remembered the carriage was one beyond. I don't know where the guard was, in the little boy's room no doubt, but Whittaker didn't need the guard, he could undo any damn door with the taste of it on his tongue. So he pulled the bolts and stepped out thirsty as a sewer— into thin air. They'd slipped the restaurant car a station or two back! Nobody missed him for hours, they thought he was sitting pretty at a barstool. And d'you know, he *was!* The engine was slowed down climbing, he fell out and bounced on the carcass of a dead sheep, got up and there right across the line was a café-place. Talk of the luck of a drunk! But it put him under the sod within the year."

Somebody began another story of three friends on their uppers who had a gay party putting the gas-poker through the milk, had the time of their lives singing and dancing, but in the end they'd all passed out, and so there was no-one to turn the gas off—but Ligne waiting for this to finish had realized suddenly what he must do. Margot had left the three risible corpses for the baby again. He drew Leslie aside:

"You'll be going on here for some time by the look of it?"

"It wouldn't surprise me. It wouldn't surprise me at all, old boy."

"Then d'you mind if I sleep in your room? If I'm up there you can make as much row as you like, and as long as you like."

"But, my lord-and-master, this is *your* party. . . . "

"I've tried, Leslie. But you know I can't drink much. And it's getting late."

Lovelace shook his head: "After all the trouble I've gone to . . . "

He lurched forward at his drink. He was at the stage when the arm no longer moves and the mouth goes forward to the glass.

"You don't seem to be having a bad time yourself," Ligne said.

"Up you go then," Leslie said. "Chuck the coats out." And then added, a shrewd look lighting his eyes: "There's a bottle of brown under the bed. My breakfast."

"I won't touch it."

"Thanking you!"

Touch his bottle of brown my foot. He's touched a bit of mine to-night. One law for the rich, another for the poor, he thought.

As he went up, Margot came down with the baby. It was beginning its gentle creaking sounds again.

"The demand seems to exceed the feed," Ligne said, happy to see this last obstacle moving away. Margot, her party over and now only an exasperated mother, grunted: "Some of that gas through his milk, that's what this baby needs." And went on down, murmuring: "Bless him."

Now he was alone at last. He went over to the window without switching on the light. From darkness he looked out over the dark gardens. Would light from a window pick out the white shape of his collar, he wondered—and moved a few inches back. The girl was still painting. Still that brilliant yellow square in a façade where all else was curtained. But now she had moved out of range, he could only see the shape of her leg lying along the floor: and this gave the room more mystery than ever; although he knew she would only be painting perhaps a skirting board, he wanted quite desperately to see her do this. He looked down at the real shadowed gardens around, the dark shapes of bushes, walls, netting, trellis and the rounded humps and feathered crests of black trees against the paler sky. Homely and sheltering, he thought, compared with that wild bare light. Yet if the light went out, how the gardens would resume their nocturnal stealth. . . .

Sounds from the party still rose. They must have opened the window now. Quite clearly on the night air there came single phrases, suddenly exploded laughter, and once the crash of glass. Moving sounds—once more he recalled the old summery echoes of his parents downstairs. And he saw, too, how the bare electric light in that girl's room took him back to kitchens long ago where he had spent happy hours with nurse and the maids. He began to ache with old longings; and these stimulated in him other yearnings—at each moment this unknown girl grew more magical for him.

I must keep her unknown, he thought. Please God, I must retain the dream. All our lives, he murmured to himself, we speak of these truths—but how often do we discipline ourselves to live by them? Now pray God I'll never meet her. Just the sight of her leg—let that be enough.

In answer the girl rose and crossed to the full centre of her stage. He leaned forward, devouring and wanting instantly more. And now he was astounded to

see that on her head she had placed a pinned newspaper, it stood up like a Redskin head-dress, dark head-
lines speckling where the eagle-black dapple of Sioux
feathers strike into white. But why not an old scarf?
Was she too poor to risk a scarf? Greedily he gathered
evidence, thinking he was getting to know her better
every moment.

Suddenly he saw by a light heaving of her shoulders
that she was talking. She was addressing a dark verti-
cal line at the back, a half-open door. She raised both
hands, gesturing someone away. Her shoulders were
shaking, she was shouting, the faint breath of a cry
came over the gardens—and then she went towards
the door pushing with her hands, pushing at air to
stop somebody who would enter. When suddenly the
light snapped off! All dark! It was as if the room and all
in it had been blown out by a sudden wind: now there
was nothing, nothing left.

He thought quickly: She had been near no wall, no
light switch. Somebody else had turned it off! What
was going on there in the dark? His knuckles whitened
on the window-sill, he shook his head from side to side,
not knowing what he could do—no doubt now, there
was violence in that room!

But then as suddenly the light came on again! No
fading on as with lime-light—it snapped on too terribly
suddenly for this small theatre. The girl was at the
door, which she had now closed and was locking.

Ligne breathed relief. He was really being too absurd. There had probably been no more violence than
a landlady's gesture—probably for economy with the

light. And the girl had refused. . . . So. . . . She had spirit. Well, he was on her side; and this suggested by a simple remove that she was on *his* side. He was over-joyed to know this.

She crossed the room, still in her Indian head-dress, and, moving very quickly, busied herself packing up paint-pots and brushes. Now how fast she seemed to move! And now, he thought, we'll see what else she'll do. Would she read a magazine or a book? Or look in a mirror? Would she play a gramophone? Studious? Vain? Sensuous? Significances ballooned.

But instead she took off the paper head-dress, folded it carefully, then carelessly threw it aside. Then crossed over to the window—reached wide, and drew two cur-tains right across them!

He stood there stupefied. Impossible! Curtains! Cur-tains in a half-furnished room! Curtains all the time . . . and a great emptiness filled him.

Into that patch of light on the crazy paving beneath Monsieur Dupont now strolled in his elegant white spats, sat down suddenly and looked alertly, salaciously round him. Modesty, Ligne thought—quite right. And it occurred to him then that never for a moment had he wondered whether she might undress in the win-dow. She was in a category removed from that.

The next day, two letters of complaint came from the houses opposite. By the afternoon post, a third. He could gather nothing from the addresses. He tried to count the houses from the back, but the terrace was

long, and error was easy. He could not be sure. He
studied the handwriting and the phrasing of each letter
carefully. One was openly abusive: the other two firm.
None pleasant. None could accurately be made to fit
any of the people he knew opposite. None of the letters
smelled of scent.

He wondered whether he might pretend that one of
them came from the girl's house? Call in with it?
Apologize. . . .

FOUR

AND ON and on it went, said Leslie later, after the inquest, after the police, after all the other events of that gusty peculiar spring—on and on and on, until I was fair browned off.

He used to sit at his window all day and look at her. Look, look, look. He put on a clean collar and a coat to look. Once she caught him looking and kind of smiled. So what does His Nibs do? Backs off his chair as if she'd grown horns and a wagger! It was the only time he left his chair for a week—when she gave him the come on!

Anyone likes a bit of a peep when occasion gives, what the butler saw, but this kind of thing's not natural. Not that you'd call old Matthew all that natural any time, what with education *and* an ulcer. Natural! Take an instance—he *gave* his money away! Not to his friends, nothing simple like that. No, he'd find someone he felt needed a lift in their lives, and there you are, slap goes a tenner. It might be an old woman he hears has never been to the seaside; or a student wants to go off to some music do: once it was a bloody girl who complained she'd never have the cash to go to the Café de Paris! He'd winkle 'em out. Nice of him, of course, but nutty all the same. And would His Nibs give a penny on a flag day? Not on your life. *That* was moral blackmail. Frightening folks with flags, that was.

So here's my Ligne stuck at his window tomming for this girl. He tried to hide it as first, used to pretend he was writing about his old lamps and stuff when I came in. I came in once too often. Anyhow, he's bursting to talk about her. Who do you think she is, Leslie? Look, she's got a new dress, Leslie! Leslie, she's growing hyacinths! He must have spent hours of my time trying to fox out a picture of her, what she did, how she lived, did she own the whole flat, and what would you say her age was? One thing we did know about her and that was how nippy on her feet she was. Once in a while old Matthew saw her pop a hat on and take up her basket—off to the shops. And out Mattie'd be and round the corner like a flash—but he never caught her, never even saw her! It's some way round the corner from ours to Mather Street, but even then she was pretty nippy.

Another funny thing—she was always alone. Sometimes she seemed to speak to someone out of the door, but no one ever came in that room. At least, once we did see a man—and you should have seen old Ligne! —but he turned out to be a plumber fiddling with a basin. Then there was a sort of shadow another time, you couldn't see all the room: but I told him perhaps it was her bedsitter, kind of private in a private flat, and it was natural for others not to poke their noses in.

Then he got worried about her get-up. She looked a simple enough girl most of the time, simple kind of frocks and her hair nice and easy—then suddenly she'd come in looking like the dog's dinner, all painted up and wearing a kind of long snaky black gown, gold bangles at her throat and hair piled up like a queen. She looked ten years older. Twenty, I'd have put her usually—and a good thirty the tarted up days. Why, why, *why?* Matthew used to rave.

That girl's a photo model, I told him. It seemed the best thing to think. But what I noticed, and Ligne didn't was she was got up that way pretty late in the day, half an hour before she pulled the curtains, say about ten or more. Then you'd see a chink of light for about another half-hour. Of course, Ligne thought this was Miss Modest getting set for her bed. But it could be she was going out, wouldn't you think? Not Ligne, of course. Dream-girl off to a night-spot? Not on your life. I never let on, in case he burst one of his vessels, poor old thing.

He used to talk about her quite openly, once we had things out in the light. After he'd skidded round the corner to get a look at her, he'd come back saying: "That's bad, Leslie, bad. I mustn't do it." You see—his real idea was to keep away, so she'd stay a dream-girl, only he couldn't help himself. Half our lives, Leslie, he said, we go all out to destroy our illusions. It's natural. But it always kicks back on us. Why can't we let well alone? Our dreams are the most valuable thing we have, and the only real innocence, he said.

You should see some of mine, I said.

Just look at all the people who dream to go to Italy, he says, and come back stung all over with mosquitoes. Far better stay at home, then they'd still have their ideal Italy. And isn't it better, he says, to think of your robin as a pretty little red-breast, all chirp and cock-eye, the pretty thing—better than to know the first thing it goes for is the eyes, peck, peck, peck with its pretty little beak? Dream and reality, he raves on—it's no highflown nonsense, the choice is there every passing second of our lives. Fortunately, he says, it's not always choice, we don't know half the time, dreams being part of reality. And where does all this get you, I ask. And tell him—stuck on a window-sill. Me, I say, I still like to know what's what.

But when you look at a sunset, he says, ten to one you're not looking at the sunset you're looking at but at sunsets you once looked at, or even sunsets you never looked at, sunsets you dreamed you looked at. Like pictures you saw long ago in one of your kid's books. So what the sunset you're looking at starts is a kind of yearning for sunsets you haven't got nor ever will have—except in your mind, that is, your old dream. Otherwise, he says, why the emotion? And that's what this girl does to me, he says. I don't suppose for a moment I'm looking at her, I'm looking at what she might have been.

Well, maybe gawping at has-beens is all right for some, if that's your unfortunate way—but I don't like to see any friend of mine getting the habit. So one fine morning I decide to find out who this two-legger is, why what and when, and bring the bacon right home to my daddy. I'll lay that if she's a nice girl Ligne'll like her reality enough.

Now first I have to find out what number she lives at. Poor old Matthew used to count the houses up and down the terrace to figure that one out. But it never works that way. What you must do is look to the roofs, pick on something high like a chimney cowl or a telly H, the one the owl sits on, Miss Tigerpants' no doubt— and just buzz round to Mather Street and look for an owl or a cowl, easy as falling off.

It turns out the house is number twenty-two. Mather Street's a long row of short brown houses with a bit of cream at the bottom and a few steps up to the door, like a million others. But what has number twenty-two done but gone right against the grain and painted itself grey all over with cheery red window-sills and door and railings. There's gold on the points of the railings and what's more there's a plaster cat covered with spots crawling flat up the wall. Brighter London.

So it's grey and red like the back where the rose garden is, the one Ligne says looks French grey and rose for France, he says. Up the front the curtains look a bit jazzy, with a lot of little faces looking through them, dolls someone's put there. Nothing else but Monsieur Dupont glaring up from the basement. Well, that's where *he* lives, anyway.

Along on the corner there's the Goat, the one Ligne calls a footman's pub for its wooden walls and what goes for plainness, though it's got pink china beer-pulls and a lot of froth on the windows—so along to the Goat I go for a pint of main line. It's not my local. So

I have to mooch around a bit, looking at the pictures
on the wall—you've got to put the landlord at his ease,
they get nervy at the sight of a new customer. What's
he doing here? they think. Is he going to waste my
time talking? Is he good for a jaw? According to their
lights. So you've got to give 'em a chance to look you
all over while you might as well study the pictures.
There's the 2nd Battalion Green Howards on what
looks like a wet Monday at Plymouth during the Boer
War; and there's a frightened looking dame in her
birthday suit paddling in a lily-pond and clutching her
charleys like the Green Howards were creeping along
the wall at her; and another two-legger with criss-cross
stockings flat out on a cushion drinking Vinayne; and a
Jewish fellow in a white suit with a saxophone signed
Morrie Morris Here's How; and a female impersonator
in a long shiny dress which says underneath, *Allow me!*
(*A lamé*) *Yours to a Cinder Dawn.* I know, I've been
back to look.

After some little time at this I go over to the counter
and lean there quietly looking at a card of aspirins. I
don't know why it is, but with all the bottles in the
world I'll always pick out the aspirins. Pub after pub
it's the same. Then a fat old dog with white eyebrows
snarls at me from underneath the bar and I say what a
nice doggie you've got to the governor who is arranging ice-cubes in a big bowl presumably for footmen,
and we get talking. After a bit I say what a cosy street
it is and number twenty-two makes a fine cheery show
and he says number twenty-two? And I says yes the
house with the red paint and he says oh, Mother

McGhee's you mean. Then we're off. It turns out she's
an ex-pro in the way of being another kind of pro these
days. Not on the proper bash, but a kind of hostess in
a dance-club. (There she goes, I think, putting that
light out. Just what Uncle Leslie said.) I ask—is it her
own house? Yes, with a tenant in the basement, he
says. Then he gives me a look and I see I've gone too
far. This bird's working out a job, he thinks, and looks
at my pockets to see the jemmy sticking out. So I'm
quick to say: "I know, fellow with green fingers."
"Green fingers?" the governor says, going pale. I put
him right on that and explain how my own garden
backs on this house, and how this fellow's a great
gardener and so on, but it takes a long long time to get
back where we were. Nervous as rabbits, these publi-
cans. Well, he says at last, you'll know Mother McGhee
then? No, I say. But you don't, I say, get to know your
neighbours much in London. Well, he says, you will
soon. She's due in any minute. In fact, she's usually
earlier than this.

This is not so hot. I don't want to seem too inquisi-
tive to the lady's face. So I thank my lucky stars when
in comes a couple of regulars and a girl to take up the
governor's time. Sandals and beards all three, the girl
wearing hers down the back, horse-tail fashion. You
might have said Artists once, but not now, not the way
things have gone. So I go off and sit down quiet in a
corner, and only then does it come to me how I'd been
so busy being clever I'd forgotten that this makes old
Ligne's dream into a fly-by-night and shall I tell him
or shall I not tell him—for if I don't then he'll go on

wasting his poor substance at the window and if I do
then you may be sure you'll hear the sound of the old
pedestal crash a mile off. To be kind and cruel, or
cruel to be kind? But who knows what you don't kill
either way?

Then in she blows. Blows isn't good enough. In she
bursts, bangs, blasts—blows us right over.

Item number one—pink hair. No lie. Pink as painted
metal, *electric* pink, pink as a bike or an ashtray at a
fair. Loud as those old girls up and down Knightsbridge with their blue rinses, only this is a *pink* rinse.

Item number two, the best pair of gams I've seen in
a twelve-month. A lovely curve of calf and nylons you
don't buy off the kerb. But what's she got stitched into
each nylon, black as a birthmark? A bleeding butter-
fly.

She's running a bit overweight. Not a lot, but she
has the bulgy look, she looks parcelled, done up with
string, only it's not string under there, there's enough
rubber and elastic and bone and steel to float a small
Zeppelin. Like a sleeping princess I saw once in a fair.
I'll never forget her. This princess was stretched out in
a glass case, eyes shut, breathing up and down like the
tide under a pier. And every time she breathed five
shoulder straps on each shoulder breathed too. She
must have been cold in there. Five slips under her
sleeping-princess outfit, each one grubby as hell, *grey*
with it; you really *believed* she'd been there a hundred
years. Well, I'll bet Mother McGhee had slips or something on her the same way. And her bottom had a kind
of false bottom following her about, a pot on a pot,

like one of those kitchen steamers. But perhaps I'm too sensitive. Anyway, working up above board, you saw how her pale blue dress and her pink hair had a face between. "Hi, Dawn!" one of the beards yells to this face as she bursts in, and the face kind of opens up like something you might see in an aquarium, a sea-plant, all pink hair and jelly, and all this slides open to say: "Wotcher!" Which is what the poor cockneys say, and very smart.

If you look closely, you could see she had two upper lips, a little one right inside her mouth under the main one. It was quite a mouth, full of pearls, two of which were like dog's fangs, real biters, one on either side. She had a good strong chin and a straight neck to hold it and her eyebrows were thick and dark. Inside all the blue she'd slapped on her lids there were a couple of eyes like old green sixpences, little and bright, dull and sparkling, and don't ask me how you get both at once. It was a big strong face, yet it wasn't really all that big—and then all of a sudden I felt I'd seen it somewhere before and I racked my nut and then I caught on: she was that male impersonator in the lamé dress in the photo! I will say you wouldn't have thought it at first, the photo being a bit hard on her. She wasn't *that* bad. In the photo she looked like a sergeant-major in a wig—but you wouldn't think that here in the Goat, you'd put her at lance-jack. And then the photo re-minded me—I'd never have thought she was the girl Matthew and I saw at the window. But now I could see how after all she could be that girl, the difference in the photo and her in the flesh showed how the length of the gardens and the window feeling might fool you just about the same the other way round, and I began remembering this and that about her and saw how it all fitted in, like a magnifying glass or the bottom end of a telescope, true and off true at one and the same time.

I wouldn't have liked old Ligne's face if she'd come round when he wrote her. After those complaints came after the party he wrote back saying "sorry," and would they all come and have a glass of wine and talk it over with him? That is, he wrote after a week beating about the bush. Wouldn't even drop the letters in. Might be seen. No, posted them. Well, got a letter or two back— but only one caller. The geezer that carries his bike upstairs every night. Said he didn't care two hoots if we blew the roof off, but it kept the lady downstairs awake—our Mrs. Peabasin—and that meant she over- slept and he got no breakfast. Well—he couldn't cycle to work on an empty stomach, could he now? *It wasn't right,* he said, *for a working man to start his day on an empty belly.* You'd think you were in church the way he said "working man." And he looks at us hard and true like a lifeboatman that has just saved the bleeding country from sinking. So all we get's this Mr. True-Blue for half an hour—and no dream-girl whatever. For which, I see now, the Lord make us thankful.

"Cheers!" she kept saying the way ladies do, and now she was in her second big gin and you saw what she was, a ginny. Not from her glass, but from the way she spoke. She never stopped. She let out these two dog-fangs and didn't even bother to move her lips but

just went on and on and on. And it sounded so tired
and weary you wondered why she bothered to talk at
all, let alone this non-stop act. In fact it was such an
unholy effort for her to keep calling up this voice from
wherever it was deep down in the rubber webbing that
she had to accent words that never needed it, and this
louder word came and went in the drone like a wave
at sea and it rocked you to sleep. And all the time her
lips hardly moved at all; so in fact you *did* go on listening, you wondered where it all came from and you
couldn't take your eyes off that mouth. It sounded like
a long, long, long-distance call droning from a red telephone left off the hook: she must have bored the heads
off bar after bar after bar with it.

What this long-distance call was about, don't ask me.
I know the word "she" came all the time, but that's not
unknown among the ladies. Sit in any busful of
shoppers and you have that "she" sshh-ing all round
you like one big mad voice sshh-ing you quiet, and well
may they "sshh," the things that come out. So it was all
about shes, and some club or other and what somebody
had said to who and what back, and I couldn't care
less, for all I cared about now was what Ligne was going to think.

First I thought it would kill him. Then I thought it
would cure him. And finally the way I looked at it,
Ligne was like a dicky old man falling in love with a
favourite disease—in time this old geezer gets so used
to his disease he really loves it. It's company, it's life—
though it's the hand of death. So when at last they
bring the doctor in and the disease goes out through

the door it's too late, the old man feels he's lost a friend, a lover, a beloved companion, and it's the loss, not the illness, he never gets over. Well, I don't want that happening to my Ligne. So I get to thinking a meeting must be arranged.

Then: "Wotcher!" Dawn yells all of a sudden. And there's a fellow putting up a bicycle on the kerb, a stiff and careful chap, neat and strong, making a kind of to-do with the clips on his trousers. And who isn't it but our old bicycle-man from opposite, the one that's saving England single-handed.

"Wotcher, Jacko!" pipes Mother McGhee at him again. And even then she doesn't bother to move her lips. But Jacko does! He lets a couple of thin rubber bands he thinks are his lips split back over a set of health-teeth made of enamel pan, his old jaw goes down shyly—and there you are, Jacko smiling, a shaft of sunlight from great Jacko who's just done an honest day's hard work, God save the Queen.

And God save old Dawn—you don't have to look a mile to see she's plain gone on cheerful Jacko. Why, she even drops her cigarette packet by mistake on purpose. And Jacko, who's just put Heavy Industry on its feet single-handed, dives for her feet like a goalie making twice the arms and legs he need because of the crowd. After which the daft sod hands her the package like it's Prince Charlie he's picked out of Virginia Water.

"You don't want to go losing them," hisses my true-blue from the corner of his mouth. Never a straight word from Jacko, always the corner, and his honest eyes are ever on the sideways shift looking for trouble, he's been in the Navy has Jacko-boy. He has a pint of mild and stands there breathing through his bottom teeth and muscling his shoulders as if it was firewater —seven-bottle Jacko, Queen of the Fairies. There he stands with his feet wide apart, legs braced back, all primed for action—which seems to be stumping out her cigarette ends like he's saved the old pub from a forest fire, women and children first—but I won't go on, that kind of holy working man makes me vomit, and I don't want my main line coming up. And anyway, I've got other worries, the lord-and-master's got to be faced with the facts, and that's going to be no picnic. However, something attempted, something done. But just as I'm getting to the door I blow old Dawn a kiss then beat it before Jacko gets me. You never know, there might be a piece of meat for Leslie on the side.

◆

FIVE

◆

Ligne was sleeping badly at the time, he spent long hours in colloquy with darkness and dawn, owls and newsboys. He would read till his eyes dropped, then put his book down carefully, very carefully, and with eyes still closed feel for the switch and turn out the light. When his eyes snapped open instantly wide-awake to the dark.

Then began the long, exhausted wait. Pressing his eyes tightly shut, he would hear sounds all the more clearly—a distant gear-change, a clock chime, tickings in the wainscot, even his own breathing. Or he would concentrate on keeping the eyes forced open to stare at the dark, which was supposed to be tiring; but on the whole the very effort woke him further. He would yawn, and the tears would lubricate his eyelids. He would try sleeping in another room—a change of bed can soothe the nerves. Or he would walk from room to room in the half-dark, guiding himself by chinks of light in the curtains, making a thunderous creaking of floorboards in the quiet. His head would cloud with an immense weariness. Too often he would peer at the luminous clock face, only to find the long drag of time emphasized; and then stand with bowed head in the middle of the floor not knowing which way next to move, his legs and his whole body aching for rest.

Finally, he would turn on the light, try to read again. But often his eyes ached with the light, and there was no book in all the house that could interest him. He would drink non-stimulants, salts or milk, until he could drink no more. He started smoking, smoked hard; and this brought on further exhaustion but no sleep. Finally he would settle on a chair or a sofa to watch the thriving night drag on to dawn.

How slowly the hours passed! At the front of the house a traffic beacon winked from along the street like a remorseless ticking clock. And at three in the morning—how heavily the town slept! He looked out and in the silence saw the houses themselves grow heavier, and he imagined inside them all the pillows, the bedclothes, all the heavy warm sleep. Once a bird cried, sharp and high, echoing dismally as it flew away. Then again there was simply the long lamplit silence. On and on the street lamps shone and the empty pavements stared silently back: the movement of a cat slinking from underneath a parked car brought unimaginable relief.

Later, at five, the first sounds. A railway whistle, a long moan from the river. Like an urgent sliding ghost, the first figure cycled by—the day's work was beginning. At intervals now there would appear more people, always alone, footsteps loud about their unspoken unwhistling passage. And the darkness began to fail, a sort of distinctness relieved the street—slowly this became a perceptible change from black to deep blue to grey, and then the miracle of the dawn's fresh air began. It was as though the eye could smell this air! The oncoming daylight showed how fresh this fogged old city could become, cleansed in one night of all its poisonous petrol and smoke. Now the air was beautifully pure, mineral and hard with the breath of empty pavements, purer by far than the grass-smelling country dawn.

Meanwhile yellow squares snapped on in bedrooms and basements, like switchboard illuminations behind whose signal lay an odour of hot morning tea against the firegrate's chill, and bedclothes thrown back still warm, and the gurgle of taps in the day's new air.

Elsewhere in the centre of the town, at seven in the morning, whole ballrooms and the restaurants of great hotels were a blaze of light! And high blocks of con- crete offices shown a million squares of shadowless yellow! Yet no movement could be seen . . . the town was alive with a bright life of ghosts. For below each window-sill grey women were crawling about the floors like slow snails, buckets slopping, brushes scrub- bing, floorbound and never appearing at window height. Grey the cleaners, grey the soap—but grey the soul? In the next half-hour, as the sky lit up and salmon clouds blazed far away over unknown suburbs the cleaners would emerge like a carnival crowd and laugh their way into buses that would take them home, work done, just as the city's true day began: a livelier

more spirited lot at that forsaken hour than anyone
you would see later in the day.

However . . . on this night in question Ligne never
went to the front of the house and the streets; his pre-
occupation led him, despite all weariness and the wish
to sleep, to the windows that overlooked the gardens:
there, as the moon rose, to resume his tired surveillance
of trees and walls and windows silvered into stone by
the moon.

It was no more than two o'clock, early as the night
went: but by now the houses were dead, the yellow
squares of living had one after another been blacked
out, only the cats and the other night-hunters were
awake.

So still in the moonlight! Yet, Ligne thought, how
voracious that ceaseless hunt in the shadows! Now
basement walls would see the edging out of big black
spiders, the flick of a beetle's mandibles, the creeping
of hard black shells along cracks in the skirting: early
in the year yet, but soon the warm months, when
night-flowers would smoulder with colour and scent
for the shade-loving moth, when even the yellow
moon's ray would give out a kind of heat—then this
life would reach a furious peak . . . what avalanches of
silent sound in the garden's quiet, what sexual screams,
what crashing of hungry jaws through carapace and
underbelly, what tearing madness for survival in the
moon's quiet heat! Yet the garden would still look a
place of peace, like a calm sea swelling above the night-
mare cries of the fish beneath.

Ligne lowered his eyes to that garden budding roses and syringa and saw how every young leaf was edged with cool, becalming light, a weight of silver foil, an engraving of leaf and light and shadow pretending a tropic exoticism . . . when suddenly he started. What had happened? . . . A large black cat, round and thick-haired, was struggling trapped on the wall. Paw caught in the netting? He strained down to see—how misted this precise engraved moonlight was!—for he knew every cat that passed. But then he saw two small whitish animals appear to each side of the cat, and suddenly the black fur swung to one side and showed itself to be not cat at all but a human face, and the white things two hands prising up on the wall, and a body now lurching after the face from Mrs. Peabasin's garden into this garden of high rose-shoots, the garden beneath his sleeping girl.

It was a man. It was a burglar.

The whole stealth of night ballooned its proportion, drew itself huge round this prowling man. He was over the wall now, noiseless, weaving his way through the maze of miniature paths, disappearing behind a bush, showing a corner of his coat, then a whole shoulder through the leaves; then he was mounting the steps to a back door.

A small window—the lattice to a lavatory?—stood open. The figure paused to study the feel of the sill, opening the window further, perhaps getting his breath.

As Ligne hurried downstairs, he wondered: Is all the house hers? But once a man is in he can climb the

stairs, enter room after room . . . and he was pulling at
the bolts in the back door and had got to the end wall
of his own garden just as the man's boots, isolated like
two shaped club-feet, stuck for a last moment out of
the window—he must have been kneeling in on the sill
—before they disappeared.

Trellis rose in Ligne's way, a brittle web of wood
plaited against his weight. Over it hung cat-wire, and
the tendrils of last year's jasmin. He had to straddle
the whole thing, it was an inch too high for his crutch,
he caught himself and the trellis heeled right over,
snapping loud like dead branch, startling the quiet gardens like a rifle shot—but he was across and dropped
quietly onto the soft earth below.

He kept dead still, watching the windows for heads,
for lights. But nothing happened. Yet . . . the other
man awake and prowling—he must surely have heard,
would he now be paused in the passage, on linoleum
dully shining in the dark, on rubber toes stepping
quietly back to see?

Suddenly a noise behind him. A cat? No, footsteps
further along the gardens. Sounds of something like
digging. The Average Husband at his marrows, he
thought. But no time to wonder about that. Ligne
snaked quickly forward along the little doll-size paths
among tall spiked plants, silvered creeper—through a
second's enchanted forest, earth and leaf-smell around
him, up to the looming high castle itself, bastioned with
a dustbin, a lavatory brush sticking from its lattice
window.

Why hadn't that brush fallen off? Or had the man

replaced it on the sill? Ligne thought suddenly: Did that man really pass through? Could he have imagined . . . ? He felt suddenly disordered, a blunderer in a private garden . . . but he was only doing what he should do . . . or should he have rung the police?

He was already on the sill, stomach pressing on the little latchpin, getting his knees up—but keeping a hand free for that lavatory brush, which now he held like a weapon. He still held it as he let himself down, wonderfully quietly to the floor—and paused breathless, listening.

Suddenly, someone tapped him on the arm. He froze, turned slowly, slowly round. Not a sound. The cistern pipes shone dull in the half-light, arrested in movement, quieter than the wall. But it was only the chain swinging almost now to a stop—the chain that must have been put into motion by the intruder himself!

Ligne carefully put the brush down, pulled himself together, and stepped out through the door into the passage. A street lamp shone through the fanlight above the front-door some way ahead. Against it, quite still, stood the shape of a man.

In that one second there raced through Ligne's mind every tense dream of how a burglar must be met. Many times he had seen this situation. First, always, how he went straight at it and knocked the man out, a surprise blow straight to the chin: and quite as cleanly the man immediately realized that Right had triumphed and allowed his arms to be pinioned. But where was the rope to bind him while Ligne went to the tele-

phone? Far better to see he was knocked senseless. But
then would he not "play possum," watch with one half-
open eye for the moment to spring up? And again, perhaps the man was armed! . . . Careful! . . . A gun . . .
no, something with a name, a Colt, a Lüger, a Webley?
. . . And to this he spoke evenly, taking care to look the
man straight in the eye: "Put it down. Don't be a fool.
You don't want to swing, do you?" But no, not a gun—
too much noise. A razor. They put razor blades along
the peaks of their caps . . . or stuck just the nicked
edge of a blade under the nail of the long third finger.
. . . So it was vital to make sure of the first blow. Jaw or
stomach? Wind him first? He might have a cosh, a
lead-weighted, wirebound little hand-stick . . . a bicy-
cle-chain like a medieval soldier's flail . . . a jackknife.
. . . Unarmed, all he could do was bunch up the change
in his pocket to make a harder fist. But at least, alone
with his suspended moment Ligne thanked God he was
not in pyjamas, undressed in nightclothes against a
burglar heavily suited and thus armoured . . . heavy
boots on naked feet . . . thin pyjamas only to cover
vital parts. . . .

But worse than weapons is the face behind the
weapon. The animal stare of concentrated hard purpose, of eyes and mouth sagged open to *do* . . . and
there were other possibilities even worse . . . worse if
this human turned beast turned coward too, worse to
watch the humiliation of capture, a man grovelling:
"Don't turn me in. . . . You've never been inside, you
don't know what it's like, guv . . . it'll be the last time,
I swear by all I hold sacred."

Trite, trite slobber—but, once alive in flesh and the dark as sickening as it must always have been, and as accusing as all appeals to mercy, bringing the burden of choice, and choice within choice, for the man might be playing for time, the knife opening in his pocket, the hand creeping to the handle of the door flung open on a ratrun escape. . . .

And if he talks of his children, of the sick at home? They always talk, someone said, they talk and talk and keep talking, sparring with words to hold time still, to weaken purpose and the impulse to action . . . suppose he accused Ligne of wealth, pointing to rich carpet and smooth cabinet, so that an old photograph in a silver frame became a sin, while at home there were those sickly bird-mouths, blue faces with dark-rimmed angel eyes, and no bread, not even bread. . . . "Why don't you get a job, then?" "Ever tried, guv? . . . just out of hospital . . . my insides. . . ."

Yet this man stood silent and still as an overcoat draped like a man! And Ligne knew he must make the initial move, move forward not over rich carpet but sliding smooth linoleum—and he did, and the man moved forward too, his face now coming into the yellow-green glare of the light, showing keen good looks and a well-shaved chin, and this was the moment when Ligne knew he must get in the first blow, hard and sure and final . . . but unused to his fists he chose instead to whisper loud: "What the hell d'you think you're doing?"

In a whisper, aware of the sleeping house above . . . yet the whisper drummed loud as a floor-board! But

louder came back the whisper from that man's face:
"And what the hell are *you* doing?"

It was like an echo, and the man's approach exactly
like his, like his own figure in a mirror, as reflections
approach silently, and he wondered for one breathless
second whether in fact he had, in the dark, come upon
some tall, strangely placed mirror.

He wondered, he *hoped,* but his hope was swallowed
up into the dark well of the stairs and the emptiness
of landings above as now this face not his own came
closer, now only a few feet away and he heard himself
whisper again urgently, commandingly: "You climbed
in the window!"

"So did you."

"You're a thief!"

The man's hand shot up, Ligne stepped back—but
the hand only placed a finger to the mouth, it made a
huge sound in the silence: "Sshh . . . " Then from the
side of his mouth, secretive: "Don't raise the bleedin'
house . . . don't gum the works."

"I'm a householder," Ligne whispered, "from opposite."

"I live next door," the man hissed back.

"Then why are you getting in windows?"

"I've got a judy."

"A . . . ?"

It was like exchanging confidences in the dormitory
after lights out.

"A judy upstairs." The finger went pointing up from
the mouth to the ceiling above. The mouth still talked

from its side. "Ain't you never had a judy on the quiet? Have a heart!"

"You're going upstairs?"

"She told me the back way, she couldn't leave the key," the man hissed.

"You mean you're visiting the lady that lives upstairs?"

"Catch on quick, don't you?"

Ligne just said: "Oh."

And then, coldly, formally, whispered: "Sorry to have disturbed you," as he turned to tip-toe away.

"No hard feelings," the man whispered, "know you're way out, don't you?"

Ligne did not answer. He took one glance at the man as, a shadow, he passed creaking softly upstairs. It was, he suddenly saw, that caller after the party, the man whom he had watched for weeks carrying his bicycle up similar flights of stairs next door. Miserably he turned away. He felt not so much absurd as wasted, as expendible . . . all his efforts of the last month useless . . . yet what efforts, when this was considered, had he made? He had mooched at a window.

And now to mooch through another window. It is sometimes easier to get in through a small space than to get out. Ligne struggled for some time in the lavatory window. But finally he did let himself down, breathing hard, a little bruised, outside. He remembered then the lavatory brush. A momentary impulse to go back and put it where it should be . . . but he shrugged it off impatiently. So she was a tart? After all that. . . .

He began his weary climb back over the trellis. Monsieur Dupont and the great ginger Persian were squatted opposite each other, faces a few inches away but turned aside, pretending not to notice each other. Both looked at Ligne resentfully; but they were a wall away and neither bothered to move as he passed—as if he were really not worth worrying about, a creature of little substance.

And those cats were largely right. For once inside, Ligne faced not only the rest of the night and the long approach of dawn, not only the loss of what he had so precariously built up, but the very insubstance of it. He sat for some time in his old chair by the window feeling what is perhaps the saddest loss of all—the loss of something one has never had. "Never!" tolls the empty heart. No sense of past surfeit comes to assuage the pain. It is like the dying of lost hopes of youth: never never will life be so beautiful, go so well, love be so true—while the heart knows that truly these things never were.

At last he could bear to look across at that blank sleeping house no longer. He had watched for a light, even a glimmer of match light. None had come. And again insubstance deepened his pain. What was going on behind that blank wall had nothing whatever to do with him—a girl he had never met with a man he knew nothing about! He went out onto the landing and into the front room. The warm winking flash of the traffic beacon shadowed a pattern on the wall every few seconds, an ionic volute from above the front porch—rose-orange fire-glow round this shadow snapped on

and off with the insistence of a water torture, and with
the terrible warmth of neon-lights still inviting gaiety
after everything in the town is shut and dead.

He felt ridiculous, too. A grown man, approaching
forty, able in mind and almost able in body, in such
distress over a kind of day-dream! He was not even ill
—the ulcer was localized, it only needed rest, it would
pass. His nerves might be upset but not irretrievably
so—worse was this lonely emptiness of heart. And in
his absurdity all the old clownish sorrows beset him;
he felt an aching impotence, and that what he was doing was laughable, and that he was playing with things
that turned to air whenever he tried to grasp them.

As the time-ticking beacon flashed and faded and
faintly lit the glass-dark windows of the houses across
the street, he fancied he saw her face in them: he tried
to make it come clearer, as one struggles for a face in
memory. And then he realized that in fact he had never
once seen her face clearly at all! Although a few days
before, with a sense of shame, he had turned the opera
glasses on her, the face that had then so suddenly approached had the negative presence of a miniature
painting, where every feature is drawn so clearly that
it mystifies, real proportions defeated by the painter's
expertise. All that he remembered about the face was
blurred and general—dark eyes against fair-coloured
hair, heavy-pupiled like liquid fruit: and again, something masculine about the face, as if it were the face of
a young man and not of a girl at all.

But a loved face is difficult to memorize. Love spends
hours on a face, devouring it—but the hunger is un-

critical; and searches beyond the face, eating at what is behind and within, never at rest, always impatient of it.

The night grew painfully, wearily on. And Ligne, tired out himself, his mouth acid with stale tobacco, his face feeling the blood drained out of it, saw at last plainly one straight and solid truth: he had been wrong not to try to meet this girl, he had been wrong to try to substantiate her as a dream in the flesh. He clenched his fists and hammered out silently in the dark room: Why didn't I? why didn't I, why didn't I? He knew that it would have been difficult to meet her: but somehow it could have been contrived.

To have, at the very least, communicated! And there alone in the night, where nothing spoke and in the deadest hours no sound came from the sleeping city, when even the last lonely traffic was over and the first not yet begun—at this hour of silence when everyone had retreated into sleep, into their private dreams, head after head after head in rows along all the streets empillowed behind walls—Ligne felt profoundly, and essentially, as if he could feel with the nails in the toes of his feet and in the little hairs at the back of his neck, this great lack of communication; he even saw suddenly how in the last day a kind of senseless hobnobbing of heads, without true communication, had coloured his life: the girl's head and his at their respective windows; Leslie's head and his own speechless over custard in the basement dining-room; the intruder's head and his own whispering in the lamp-lit linoleumed hall; even the two cats, inches between their noses, on the wall. All heads at each other, no true communication.

And as he thought back he remembered Leslie, poor old Les, whom over the custard he had sworn to take steps about. Steps? Vaguely he had thought, perhaps, of getting rid of him. Simply because he wanted the room upstairs! Could he really have sacked Leslie? Drained of purpose, he looked back on himself earlier that day as at a drunken representation of himself: he could not now imagine the unremembered fever that must have flooded him.

Greyness began to fill the sky, and the first workers plodded by. Then the sound of a horse's hooves came clattering in metal-shod rhythm, *one*-two-three-four; past lampstandards, iron railings, past pavements already worn smooth in the last century—in a moment sixty years had vanished and the sound alone put him back within a London he would never have and now wished for, like all last hopes, desperately.

He got up and though usually he moved quietly at night, stamped into his sitting-room and began carrying books, papers, pens into the front bedroom. He had done with that garden room. To and fro he went, bringing all the impedimenta of the day into this new sphere, piling things everywhere.

The first birds woke and then, as if these had been instruments tuning up, the whole orchestra began. The flash of the beacon on the wall faded in the growing dawn light. An electric milk cart whined by. Bottles rang glassily on doorsteps. The day had begun.

At eight o'clock Leslie came down with the tea he

made upstairs on a ring, to find Ligne stretched on his bed, dressed, in a litter of books, and at last asleep. The curtains were undrawn.

"Hallo, hallo, *hallo!*" Leslie said to himself, and quietly withdrew.

◆

SIX

◆

LATER THAT MORNING Ligne completed the transference of his things from the back room.

At first he decided to keep silent on the events of the previous night. But finally, both because some explanation was necessary to Leslie, who was no fool, whose mournful considerative eyes would see through any fabrication, and also because the pure wish to tell someone was greater than the fear of ridicule—finally he gave Leslie an outline of what had happened. He took an ironic tone towards himself; and thus made communication again incomplete.

"So now," Ligne ended, "I'm going to be strict with myself. Application, discipline. A front-room boy."

"Making a complete ass of yourself, if you ask me," Leslie said. "Perhaps you'll take my advice next time and go in and get the lady."

A pause, and then he said: "As a matter of fact, it would have been a bad move. You wouldn't have liked her. I've met her."

"What!" Ligne swallowed immediate anxiety. He felt affronted. And the night might not have occurred.

"She's a kind of tart," Leslie went on, and described to Ligne's unbelieving ears her gross detail.

"No," Ligne said, "No. She looked so—so young, for instance."

"Butterflies on both stockings," Leslie repeated, "big black butterflies."

"Well," said Ligne, "why not?" To his surprise he was still on the girl's side.

But on and on Leslie went, rubbing it in, describing Jacko too, until at last Ligne was convinced; and began for the first time to feel relief that he had escaped something.

"So that's that," he said.

And somehow, perhaps because of a certain relief, the house settled down for the morning.

Old Fosdyke called for another session on the monograph, and quite by chance added to the air of disillusionment. That morning some trouble with his corns had forced him out of his beloved sandals, which chafed, into boots—and disturbed by this he forgot his resolution to humour Ligne. So that when Ligne, remembering the sound of horses' hooves in the early morning, expatiated on the past glories of horse traffic, Sir Hugh exploded.

"Horses my foot!" he said, his pale old baby-face reddening in doll-patches, "they made fifty times more noise and smell and bother than any of your motors. Jingle jangle, thump-thump, falling over, running away, pump-shipping and doing number two all over the road, if you could call it a road. More like a bog in my day. You've never seen traffic jams like it—cab drivers slashing each other with their whips! And half your ostlers drunk—you used to give your servants small beer then, they called it small but it was stronger than any *you've* ever had—"

"But think of the smell of petrol! Don't you realize uncle, that every motorist suffers from slight carbon-monoxide poisoning—"

"And do *you* realize, sir, what it is to smell horses, horses, horses, day in day out? When every confounded street stank of them, harness and hay and sweat and their you-know-what, whinnying and falling down, rolling their horrid eyes—no, me for a motor any day. They haven't got those long yellow teeth, either," added the old man with a smile, revealing his.

He paused for breath and added more kindly: "You think the past was all roses, Matthew. I suppose it's natural. We like to forget pain, remember the good things. Mankind always dreams of a golden age he'll never have."

"Didn't you?"

"No. Well—in early youth perhaps. But it was cut short."

"How?"

The old man looked at him sharply. Shook his head. Then sighed: "Well—it's common property now. Hardly need prevaricate. By your mother, of course."

This always made Ligne feel uncomfortable. A sanctimonious shadow seemed to fall about the room despite the pathos of an old man's lost love.

But Sir Hugh went on softly: "It was hopeless to hope for her. She was married and in love with her husband, and that was that. That was that for forty years. So I had my unattainable golden age to hand every time I visited them—golden age for luncheon or tea or dinner. But at least it was limited to her, to the one person, and I was able to get moving on other things. It was a kind of pest canalized."

"And now?"

"These things come to an end. They work themselves out of you. I've ceased to wish for her. I suppose she rather wants *me* now, that's the way of it."

Ligne said: "I'm half your age. I don't like to think of the thirty years ahead."

A look of impatience, a crow's shadow crossed the old man's face.

"Dreaming's no good," he snapped. "Something hopeless about it. Who was the fellow said hopelessness attracts hope? What you want is to *be* hopeless. You need a real knock. Six of the best laid on the hard way."

Ligne was saying slowly: "Perhaps I've had it," and hearing the sententious phrase, was thinking, "There I go again"—when there came a sharp tap-tap-tap on the door, a knuckly woman's tap, and the tastefully painted face of Mrs. Orme, above a smart silk scarf printed in soft Italian colours, showed itself.

"Mr. Lovelace," said Mrs. Orme, "wishes to see you. Actually it seems urgent, judging by the *fracas* he's up to."

There was a pause, as if more should somehow be said. Ligne had never quite got used to Mrs. Orme. Every time she bent with a brush and pan he was

mentally on his knees to help her. She was a mysterious sign of the times, of a revised economy of the
classes. She worked extremely hard for the very small
sums he paid her—yet had once excused herself early
because of a cocktail party she was giving, at another
time to dress for the theatre, and on numerous occasions she was called for by a "friend" in a larger car
than Ligne could have afforded.

"Thank you, Mrs. Orme," Ligne said politely, his face
pulled grave, as if he were addressing a lady shop-
walker. When Leslie came thumping down the stairs,
weaving from side to side on his thin knock-knees,
stamping his flat feet and shouting: "Quick! There's
two!"

"What?" Ligne said.

"There's *two!* Two for the love of Mike! Come on!"

Mrs. Orme shrugged her shoulders: "Well, *really!*"
she smiled, shaking her head sadly. But Leslie had got
Ligne by the sleeve and was dragging him through
the door to the landing and the back room.

"Pon my Sam," muttered Sir Hugh coming after
them, an eager fire lighting his eyes.

"Well," said Leslie in the other room, "what about
that?"

At the window opposite, not one but two women
with fair hair leaned side by side on the sill. The morning sunlight flashed on glass, on a bracelet, on teeth
smiling. Beneath, a man bald as a marble cannon-ball
pressed a brass nozzle quietly to his roses: all was at
sparkling peace, the night might never have been.

Matthew felt he was involved again in some complex

binocular vision. They looked so much the same. But somehow of different proportion, of inverted detail. One seemed to be in focus, the other not. Both the same and different, like twins that were not twins, young mother and old daughter, a couple of girls dressed as sisters in the music hall . . . some such uneasy duality played about the figures, one, two, in the single stage of the morning-bright window. Both girls must have had double crowns to their heads—their hair was piled high, and at first glance they looked like two Marie Antoinettes, two marionettes.

Backing behind a fold in the curtain to look harder, he saw that one was young and pretty, the other a few years older and heavier. He saw plainly that it was the younger one he had regularly seen in that room. Yet the other bore such a blurred, weighted resemblance! The younger had tan-gold hair, the older one pink—yes, quite definitely pink. Both had a darkness about the eyes—with one it was make-up, but with the other her own dark brown, plum-broad pupils. Both had firm cheeks, dark thick eyebrows, and an erect set of the neck: there was indeed a tone of masculinity in each, though while the elder looked like a man with a wig, the other looked more like a boy, or a young girl masquerading as a page.

"My mistake," said Leslie.

Ligne shook his head impatiently. "Nonsense. But why didn't we ever see them together before?"

"Perhaps it's her room and she keeps it private. People do."

"But when she was out? Did the other ever come

in?" An appalling sensation of betrayal: "Did I ever look at the other thinking it was *her?*"

"It seems," said Leslie, "old pink-mop owns the house and lets the basement to Baldy down there squirting. That's what I gather. So why shouldn't she let a room upstairs too?"

Ligne suddenly remembered: "We saw her pulled back. Remember?"

"Takes someone closer than a landlady to do that, takes a friend," Leslie said. "Or d'you think it's her mum?"

"It *can't* be her mother—no, I won't have it. . . . "

Over the gardens the two women had suddenly burst out laughing. They were hanging on the sill helpless, clutching their stomachs with the sill. Bits of washing, a handkerchief or two and a scarf, had been strung on a little line under the window. Now the scarf had been whisked off by the wind and had flown out and then slowly sunk like a balloon onto the top of the syringa bush below. It lay decorating the flowerless budding leaves like a giant red hibiscus. The two women laughed like anyone laughing at sudden upset. The bald man aimed his syringe at this bright big new flower, pretending to squirt, and they laughed all the more.

As with the tree surgeon—again easy laughter! But not only a moment's envy clouded Ligne's world, clouds too clouded it—that little wind that had blown down the scarf was the presage of rolling slate stormclouds that now came flooding over the housetops as fast as ink through blue blotting-paper, racing, turning all dark—and now the white cornices of houses shone as if lit from within against this great slate mass above, and people must have felt within them atavistic terrors, imminence of the Last Trump. There in the garden the bald man turned his bald face to the sky, Mrs. Peabasin in the next garden stood transfixed, looking up, her scissors half-cut through a clutch of creeper; perhaps half-a-dozen people within sight were struck in attitudes of stone surprise at this ordinary phenomenon of an English spring. Only the Average Housewife had moved instantly into action, already she had half her washing off the line, her mouth was stuffed with pegs and she threw more of these recklessly to the ground as she clutched at her white lovelies, her nappies and towels, to hustle them in beneath smiling skirts of safety.

Big single splashes dropped as from a leaking ceiling. And then the sky black all over broke, white hailstones fell dizzying as the lines on a television screen, big hard ice-blobs bounced all over the paved gardens scattering cats, ringing on tin, drumming the gutters full, finally to lie drifted on paving and grass like the white confetti of blossom one might have expected at this time of year.

Hailstones on his bald head had sent the man with the pest-syringe running in—and now those two twin women with a wondering final shriek, half-laughter, half-terror, had slammed down their window and were gone. Ligne and Leslie found themselves looking over gardens and houses desolate, deserted, dark. The brightness of morning, the flash of golden locks at the window—how could these have been? The whole day had snapped out like a light at night: a dishwater drabness, drained of all light, gave the darkness the look of an old blurred photograph. The hail had turned to dark steady rain, and ominously from the clouds above an airliner drummed in flying low, very low indeed, unseen.

Ligne still stared at the blank deserted window. A lazy light-headed tiredness from the night still held him, making everything seem more simple than it was. "Where did you meet her—the older one?" he whispered.

"She goes to the Goat," Leslie said. "But I didn't actually meet . . . "

"In the evening?"

"Seven, about."

Ligne looked suddenly blank: "Why don't we go there this evening?"

Leslie raised his eyebrows. "Why not?" he said. The lord-and-master was certainly going it!

Sir Hugh opened the door and stood eager in his grey shorts, head poised listening to the aircraft drum-mining: "Four-screw job—probably a Viscount . . . you chaps were certainly quick off the mark . . . up the rebels, eh?"

The aeroplane thundered more faintly away, nosing blindly to some awful pilot's fate.

"Two of them," Ligne muttered. "All done by mirrors."

"Eh?"

Mrs. Orme entered. "Hailstones round your dogs, Mr. Lovelace," she announced.

They all looked at her in silence. Life, with difficulty, was trying to resume itself.

"I thought you'd like to know," said Mrs. Orme, "actually." And as still no one spoke, she withdrew, expressing affront by no more than a shoulder slightly raised, as a mannequin might turn, or a large bird flex its wing.

The three men watched the door close in silence. Then they stretched, breathed. Lights were now seen switching on here and there over the storm-dark façades. Ligne glanced out, smiled, and looked back into the room.

"Let's all have a drink," he said.

◆

SEVEN

◆

TOWARDS EVENING, the rain stopped and out came a golden watery sun. The sky turned to violet and gold, wet walls blushed patches of rose and pink never otherwise seen, puddles blazed purple in the worn grey pavement, and Ligne and Leslie sauntered out into this fresh, life-popping after-rain air together: Leslie swaying eagerly on his knock-knees, one step this way, one step that, a thin moustached metronome in grey bags—and Matthew, tall and thoughtful, a little bowed, a man in a suit, the suit walking, with somebody grave and abstracted somewhere within.

Curtains blew out of newly opened windows. There was the opening and shutting of front doors that follows rain. Cars wooshed water-spray on the wet macadam, and the whole evening glinted with fresh life, like a new day beginning: yet sacerdotal, purple and gold.

And so it was, Leslie said, that seven o'clock found me and Master propping up the bar of the old Goat, thirsty work.

The Green Howards and the lady-paddler and old Morrie Morris and so on were all there on the walls still. I pointed out that lamé business to Mattie, to see how he'd take the look of Dawn McGhee. He never recognized her. It was what a photograph does, giving a kind of difference, like a news photograph, like a person in a window come to that. He told me *à lamé* and allow-me was a joke, the way you said it, and My God I saw it at last. This depressed me. I found myself looking at those aspirins again.

But I didn't let on it was Dawn. From now on, I thought he's got to take what comes. I didn't relish it, but there—at least the Master had come out of his hole. It's funny how I'd rather see him take a knock or two than see him like he was. But that's the way with people and their friends—they like to see them alive and kicking however much it hurts, once they drop away you've lost them and that's too bad. Nice and friendly of people.

The pub began to fill. . . . As I said—a little pub, all planked wood with the knots carefully drawn in, and all along one wall, between the GENTS MIND THE STEP and the door with the old goat frosted in the glass— all along the wall was a wood seat. People sat on this in a row, glasses in hand or on the little ledge just above their heads, balancing glasses on their nappers you might think when you'd had one or two. But sitting up straight-backed against the wall they looked more like a row of citizens at night-school. And at school that night we had, reading from door to Gents, a thin fellow in a bowler hat with a red-white-and-black face all in patches, black moustache and eyebrows and dolly-red cheeks; two old girls with blown-up legs that made you ache, clutching their purses in one hand and their stout in the other; a couple of young soldiers, poster-health as thick as paint on their faces; and Matthew and me.

Up at the bar, the beard and sandal gang again with their girls in trousers and the thin little black slippers you wanted to stamp your boots on. "Not a footman among them," I said to old Matthew, "unless you count the chap with the red-white-and-black face, and we don't want to see *him* in green velvet." "I only said it was a footman's pub in the *past*," Ligne sighs. "The past, the past, the past," I say, "it's like a plague with you." "Nag, nag, nag," he says, "you old cow." And so on. Friendly talk. Never a moment's rest. And down goes the beer and up goes the smoke and everyone talks louder, the old pub grinds its pistons and gathers up speed for the down-hill run to Primrose Junction— and then like a pink bomb in blows Dawn McGhee. In her blue again, a colourful sight, Came the Dawn and no error.

She goes straight into action. "Wotcher!" she cries to the landlord. And then: "Coughing better?" to one of the beards who's just choking on his cigarette . . . and it's a second or two before I dare look round at Matthew. He's gone dead white.

I cannot do much more than let this soak in. It's the knock, and it had to come. But I take care we soak in something else at one and the same time, so I keep on ordering up and old Matthew puts them down with a will. Still, I think, this is only Mother McGhee, it's not *his* girl, but all the same it's a nasty knock. Meanwhile the old pub's filling up and soon we have a real brown buzz going. You can't see the old yellow ceiling for smoke and what with the brass and the glass and the old floor thumping and everyone saying pardon me and spilling their beer about, why the whole brown pubful is getting cosy as a fat man in a full room. One of the young soldiers gets up and obliges with a ditty, Put Away Your Tweezers Till Our Eyebrows Meet Again, and old Matthew pours more gin on his ulcer to drown the sound, and then I hear Dawn scream above all this din that her club is called The Acacia Room, Arse-arsia to some, she shrieks, though we don't get many like that these days. And now you should see her up on her stool tossing her pink head and laughing, laughing, laughing, her pretty little fangs champing the air and loving it, and there's her bag taking up most of the bar and round her like a circle three or four of the boys— two of them the beavers, also a man I don't know in a blazer. Well, you see them everywhere, painted ladies perched in pubs. There's always a lot of the hail-brother about them, they're really on man's brown territory even in this day and age and this makes them a bit jumpy, a bit too *jolly*, a bit *equal* for God's Sake. And naturally old Dawn looks twice the man the others look, even the men. Dawn's only trouble is she can't see her butterflies from where she's sitting and it gives you the willies to see her twist to look down at them, there'd be a ripe old bang if her stays went. Meanwhile she's putting away the gin, and all around the mirrors are flashing and we're all sitting watching with glasses on our heads, and the old dog with white eyebrows is now let out to waddle about looking sorrowful at people, and the man with the red-white-and-black face suddenly rises, takes off his bowler, and pipes from under his black moustache: "I will now oblige with The Irish Chiropodist's Song—Your Fate is in my Hands," and sits down again, never a smile, all very grave and funnycuts. And this brings a good old giggle from the two old girls with big legs, whose purses and stouts seemed to be weathering very nicely, which shows how wrong you can be, right enough.

And Ligne's a changed man tonight, got the devil in him. "Come on, Les," he says, grabbing my sleeve, "do your stuff."

It took me two minutes.

You might say that's two too long with a girl like Mother McGhee; but you've got to know how to handle them. It's a matter of a password, and it's got to be the right one. Get the right password and you put people at ease—if you say anything original you're done for. There's a pass for most occasions. If you're alone up against the lavatory in this pub and a stranger comes in and sets up beside you, the silence, if you can call it a silence, gets uneasy. There's you and this chap beside you all alone in a little room standing against a wall and looking up at the pipes. Strangers. Not introduced. No one likes this for long. So what do you say? "What goes in must come out," you say, and the other fellow smiles like a well-canaried cat. He knows you're regular. The business in hand—that's another one, "the business in hand"—can be continued with easier hearts all

round. There are men saying this to each other in lava-
tories all over town every minute of the day, no error.
And what do you say if you're on a railway platform
and the barometer's five below? "Hot enough for
you?" you say. And that breaks the ice nicely, thank
you. Or how about when you've let fall a naughty
word in front of the ladies: "Pardon my French!" They
like it. "Enjoy your trip?" says a bus conductor when
you fall flat on your fanny, and this particular password they also call cockney humour, *perky*, you can't
keep a good cockney down and I'll say you can't, the
loud-mouthed bunch of bouncers, ripe gutta percha
the lot.

So what about Dawn?

Ordering what is called a nice ice-cold lager from the
bar just by where she's sitting, the line is to take a swig
of the cold beer and shiver out loud to old Matthew:
"Brrr—freeze the balls off a brass monkey."

And then look startled but kind of mischievous at
Dawn with a "Pardon my French" just for old time's
sake.

It works like a charm. Try it next time you meet a
lady.

Dawn gives a light little laugh with her two miles of
shark's teeth. She knows I'm regular; she's heard it before; she knows it's Very Funny; and now she opens
her mouth further to show she catches, the clever
thing: "Hot enough?" she says.

From then on it's off.

Of course I've got old Matthew with me dolled up
like the dog's dinner so it's all the easier for that. And

now while I keep up the main flow Matthew sticks out
a creepy old feeler from time to time. "What a big
house you've got, Mrs. McGhee. Don't tell *me* you live
there all alone?" And Ligne's old teeth stay fixed in a
smile right across his face as he takes the full force of
Dawn's simper, for of course she thinks he's mad for
her. "Well I've got a lodger down below," says Dawn,
"They call me Mother McGhee the Landladee." And
off she goes into hoots at this, for apparently there's
something a little sporty about having a "lodger."

And Ligne hoots with her. He hoots beautifully. I'll
say this for my Matthew, he hoots away and then he
raises a waggly finger and shakes it right in her puss:
"And no one else, no one at all?"

And Dawn says casually, for there is hardly a hoot in
such news: "Only my kid sister."

"Kid . . . ?" begins Ligne. Then a kind of electric
flash goes bang in his eyes, what is what has sunk in—
but praise be he manages to go on hooting: "Well, well
—and how old is *she?*" he says, with a wicked leer.

"Sweet twenty-one-key-of-the-door!" says Dawn.

And you should see Matthew's eyes, dreamy as the
eyes of a man doing mental arithmetic, fitting it all together. Would the sister speak with Dawn? Dress like
Dawn? Take, in fact, after Dawn?

And then what does that Ligne do? He drops the
subject of the sister absolutely and utterly!

Now there's a clever, I think. After four weeks with
this one thing in mind—it's a miracle of self-control.
And now what he does do is make out it's only Dawn
for him, asking who she is and what she does, all with

a real old-fashioned glint in his eye—but all he's really
getting at, the old fox, is what her house is like inside.
When she says this room's here and that room's there,
and the staircase is so and the bathroom thus, he says
well our staircase is there and the bathroom so, and
this room's here and the other's there—and isn't it extraordinary, as the houses should be the same, and on
and on he goes until Dawn, who isn't that interested,
has finally to burst out, for no girl with butterflies on
her legs is likely to discuss Home Planning for long:
"Well for God's Sake come and see for yourself!"

"Well—*thank* you," says Ligne, cool as a whistle, "I'd
love to. When?"

"For crying out loud when the pub shuts if you like,"
snaps Dawn. "Come up and have one while we change
for the club. But for *Gawd's* Sake take it easy now."

"We?" says Ligne.

"Liliane and me."

"Liliane?" says Ligne.

"My sister, for heaven's sake. Now can't we talk
about something else?"

"Yes," says Ligne, slowly now. For the first time you
can see he's taken one hard. That kid in a night-club,
he's thinking.

But even then I'll give it to him for he adds: "I'll
bring a bottle," with the courage of a man facing a
nasty operation, gravel perhaps.

Dawn then lets drop how she's training Lily—sorry
she says, Liliane, that's her new business name she
keeps forgetting—training Liliane to be a dancing part-
ner at the old Arse-arsia like herself. "What!" says

Ligne, and Dawn looks a bit odd at him and repeats herself, and Matthew says quite loud, "But you *can't* send a girl like that into *that* sort of work!" "*What* sort of work?" says Dawn a look growing in her eye, and I don't like the look of this look so crash goes the old glass on the floor by mistake on purpose and everyone looks down at their boots and sandals and skirts and butterflies. But no harm's done and a broom comes over the bar and I have a chance to whisper to Matthew "Go easy" while I'm bent over sweeping. Yet I don't need to worry—for now we have other diversions. The geezer in the blue blazer, for a start. This one's a straight-up clean-limb with a great gruff moustache. He likes to look fierce, the old spaniel, and now he ups and does his favourite trick. This is simply to point to his empty glass and frown at the landlord, shake his head sorrowfully, look grim at the landlord and follow the landlord about with his eye as if he is *such* a naughty boy not to have filled it without being asked. Blazer does this *every time* he has a drink, he's done it *every time* in *every pub all* his life, year after *year, every* time he has a drink. A bit stale by now? Not to Blazer. And there's another thing about Blazer, his beer's always flat. No top, he complains, shaking his old nut. I could give him a bit of inside guff there— because it's the oil from his handle-bars does it and no fooling. But I won't. Old Blazer'd never believe it, not Blazer.

And he's not the only comedian around, no, here's old red-white-and-black face, old flag-puss, getting up again and saying: "My next number will be a Loving

Song of Tryst and Trrrust—Hernia, you're Mine." And this is now too much for the old stout-and-pursers for one of these gets up and kicks a swollen leg, screaming "Knees up Mother Brown!" and the landlord yells "Hey, no dancing, singing yes but dancing no, no dancing licence here," and so old flag-face mutters soon there'll be pubs for drinking through the left side of your mouth and other pubs for the right side so help me. "What the hell time's closing here?" he adds fiercely.

He gets his answer pat, does funny-cuts, for the governor yells back, "Last orders please!" straight in his teeth and you'd think that that would be enough for the company present, but no, every man and beast there has to look up at the clock and shake their heads. And then there is the little silence, like a sorrow, while they all empty their drinks to try and get another one in before Time. But thankfully all this had made Dawn forget what old Ligne said, and she's now going crazy saying "Down the drain" one side and "Bottoms Up" the other and stuffing about in her bag a couple of bob to buy a last one, which Matthew cleverly forestalls, buying this and a bottle too. Then suddenly he goes white again, and quickly orders himself an extra double. It's his ulcer kicking. But he sinks his gin. He's out to kill it.

So there's the whole pub thrashing down its last drinks, the governor pulling on his beer-handles like a crazy signalman with a runaway express—and the doors bang wide and the bolts crash down and there are more yells of Time and the bar-cloths are flapping—

and there we are out in the street with Dawn clacking ahead on her high steppers. The skirt in trousers and her beavers have scented the bottle, and old Blazer of course, and it's all a bit mixed, what with the night-air and the pavement swinging but sooner or later we're up in Dawn's room, sitting about on a bed and a sofa and chairs, sniffing like boozy old dogs at this new and astounding place it's got us to.

Dawn's room got stuck way behind the times. Old Dawn has a litter of pink fringed lampshades and dolls from the roaring twenties: there's pierrots and Dubarrys and Sorbo-pups, orange and black cushions and blowsy pink satin curtains and plenty of lace behind—it might all be what some sentimental old vaudeville queen gifted her when she first hit the Town, a sweet and painted seventeen. The place stinks of chypre, and everything's shaded, dark heads against dark pink lights, it's all a bit intimate in a blowsy, sexy way. And you felt there was an unemptied chamber-pot under the bed—but it might have been the chypre.

No sooner settled and sniffed, the beards and old Blazer begin carrying on fit to burst. *Mackerel,* they talked about in the dark pink shade! "Why, it's the finest fish of the sea!" gruffs Blazer. "Dirty eaters," shakes a beard. "All manner of sewage, and the dead, the drowned too." At which Blazer gives a great snort: "Pfaw! Old wives' tale!" "Look at Cornwall," nods the beard, "running with mackerel. And why? Because there's not a cove on the coast doesn't come in for a tasty piece of drownded caravaner." "That's it," the other beard says to Blazer, "no use boning a mackerel.

There's always the odd bits of bathing suit to get in your teeth."

Yes, we are all no sooner settled and chatting when there is a whispering out there in the passage, and Matthew's face is set as a grave, and now I know This-Is-It, and sure enough in she comes.

She's a smasher.

She's young and clean and sweet, you can smell the soap with your eyes, and she says good evening quietly and natural as a princess.

Not a trace of old Dawn in her—except for that creepy likeness about the face. And her voice is soft and grave, you might say humble if it wasn't for a look in her eye, which is knowing and clear, wise as the eye of a straight child.

As she comes into the light, if you can call it the light, Dawn shrieks: "Why Lil, you haven't changed, dear!"

"You said it was our late night," Lil says, "I thought I'd wait."

"Late night yes, but not late like this!" And Dawn turns to explain: "We have late nights at the Acacia when some of the girls don't come till the place fills up, there's not the need really—"

And the beards' judy in the trousers says understandingly: "No there wouldn't be the need really, would there?" A bright girl.

So Dawn says again she'd better change now, but then asks Liliane if she hadn't better have a drink first to pep her up.

"I don't think I will, thanks," says Liliane and Dawn

says go-on-you-must and Liliane smiles and shakes her head but nevertheless Dawn pours a snorter and puts it in her hand. "Now you do just as I say," she says and the girl takes a sip and shudders, and then looks over at Dawn like a child asking not to have to eat her sago or something.

"Now now none of that! Just you drink it up, miss, this isn't a morgue!" And the girl quietly obeys. But she hasn't lifted her glass before Matthew's voice comes out fair and square: "She doesn't have to," he barks, "if she doesn't want." He was back in the dark when Lily came in, I hadn't liked to watch him but this voice showed how worked up he was, it would've cut holes in a battleship let alone old Dawn, who spins round quick as lightening: "Oh? Really?" she says.

Matthew repeats: "You can't *make* a girl drink like that."

"And who in hell d'you think *you* are? This is my house, I'd have you know." Very cut, she is. Dawn is a girl who gets cut easy, the thickest skin being the thinnest.

Ligne was icy polite: "That's a very strong drink," he says, "you can't *force* people. . . ."

And old Dawn's hands go on her hips, she puts her legs astride and her whole chest out and hollers: "If I think," she hollers, "my kid sister wants a drink, then a bloody drink she's going to have."

At which Ligne takes a step to meet her: "And if I think. . . . " he begins, cold, his face grave as sin in that pink light, when: "There!" says Lil who has quickly

tossed back the drink, "please don't squabble over me.
Thanks, Dawnie, I suppose I needed it. And thank you,
Mr.—I don't know your name," she smiles nicely at
Matthew, "for being so solicitous."

That stopped them both in their tracks. You could
see anyway that Dawn hadn't properly taken to
Matthew. He'd hooted and done his best—but he'd let
himself go too much in the pub, he hadn't watched his
voice and what kind of words he said, and some of
these were far above Dawn's head, and that always
gets them, they think a rise is being taken, snobbish
they think and they get the needle and this makes them
want to hit back. And there's nothing to hit back
against, and then they're twice as mad.

Then I notice Lily. She's looking at Matthew with a
look in a million. You'd know it a mile off. I don't know
why—it may have been Matthew's kind word on her
behalf—but it's plain as God's great pikestaff she's stuck
on Matthew, she kind of shines as she looks at him.
And for another thing she recognizes him. "Why, you're
the man from opposite," she says standing there bang
in front of him. There at last, with her thick dark eyebrows making a kind of fun of her eyes, which are
dark too, like an animal's, a squirrel's or something,
and her blonde hair.

Which is the perfect cue for the door to open and let
in who else but True-Blue Jacko.

At least it diverts Dawn. "And where have *you*
been?" she asks all fangs again. Smiling.

Jacko waggles his great jaw. "Just taking a bit of a

nap, y'know," he says casual, as if he's swum the Channel and back, "got to be up betimes in the morning, y'know."

"Oh in the bedroom?" Dawn says, not waiting for an answer, as she pilots him towards the gin-bottle.

And I hear Matthew's mind thundering: Great Lord, what bedroom?

But I hear him saying to Lil: "Yes, I live opposite," and stopping dead.

And then what? He simply turns away from her. Flat. Leaving her standing after all these weeks!

But I know him. I know Mattie—it's not just that "bedroom." It's his perverse streak, it's a damn great dreadful thing that comes over him when everything's going well. He just can't stand straight talk or fair weather. It's a kind of shyness.

To some extent Leslie may have been right. But for Matthew Ligne in that chattering dark-faced room of chypre and pink silk curtains, at the end of such a strange day and night, tired but exhilarated—sensations played much deeper than any shy wish to be perverse. It was something in the very presence of Lily herself that bred in him real and immediate antipathies.

She was indeed like the girl he had seen in the window—and at these close quarters even more attractive. And indeed when she first appeared framed in the dark doorway from the passage, Matthew's heart had leapt, his stomach had swallowed. But then she advanced into the room: stepped out of her bubble intangibility

into an immediate presence. And simply by being
there, she had broken his dream. She was indeed like
the girl in the window, except for one vital difference
—she was in the room, not in the window.

He could see, even in that dark-pink light, the little
blonde hairs along her real arm: he could feel the
young delicacy of her skin, so near now that he could
imagine the small fresh odours that must breathe from
it: he could now actively sense the space she occupied
in the room: and her lips curled back in a smile showing wetness on her teeth, and through the wetness
issued words and from the words personality . . . she
was real, with real demands.

He was tired from his sleepless night. He had drunk
a fair deal. And now, by a miracle, by chance, his
dream had come true! Yet . . . what had she come up to
but expectation, what had she fulfilled but exactly the
dream itself? She had crossed from one dimension into
another: descended to earth from the wonderful wings
of hope: deserted the freedom of his mind for flesh and
time and reality. The dream was broken. All that can
be said is that the girl was lovely, in all appearances
"perfect"—and so the bottom dropped out of Ligne's
little world, making him turn away, frowning, from
the girl with whom he was undoubtedly in love to
speak of mackerel with a bearded stranger.

"After all," Matthew snapped, "we eat dead fish,
don't we? A dead fish is a corpse."

"That's different," said Blazer. "After all," he added.

"We meet again," said a new voice out of the side of
a mouth.

The burglar in the passage! Matthew, so muddled, remembered him coming in a few moments ago now from this other upper passage of bedrooms. Old doubts came rushing up. From the moment he had seen two women at the window, this girl he knew now as Lily had been exonerated—yet now again he had to think: Where was the man "resting" while Dawn was out in the pub this evening, on whose bed and with whom?

"Keep it dark," hissed Jacko's dark head. "Pals, eh?" he added with manful meaning. In the dark Ligne saw a great wrestling movement about his face, Jacko's jaw working. "Of course," was all he could think to answer as he strained his eyes, not only against the room's dark but the dark muddling his mind—to see more clearly Jacko's strained and big-boned face, eyes sunk in a kind of coaldust of graven labour. He sat stiff upright on a backless stool, awkward in such company, pretending enormously to be at ease. Ligne felt abruptly sorry for him—for one close look at the man had removed the possibility of an association with Lily. What a cross this addiction to Dawn must be!

"Liliane indeed!" he swore under his breath, and suddenly furious at her, one moment jealous, the next angry, he turned to look for her again—and his heart rose, for once more she stood away in the doorway, framed, remote again as in her window, and all his wild wonder returned as, with Dawn, she left the room.

"She's gone to dress her up," said Jacko. "Poor kid."

"Why poor kid?"

"Not that it's none of my business."

"What do you mean, poor kid?" Ligne said fiercely.

"Well see for yourself," said Jacko, "when she comes back. It's not right, not to my way of thinking, the way she dolls that kid up and where she takes her to. A kid like that."

"You seem to be well in with it all, yourself," Matthew said.

"I've told her straight what I think, don't you worry," Jacko hissed, his lips pressing thin on a hundred-and-ten commandments. "I don't hold with any of it, not as it concerns Dawn neither."

"But you and Dawn—"

"Now I don't want no insinuation," Jacko hissed playful, suddenly raising in mock horror big bushy eyebrows beneath one of which the eye then closed in a long, conspired wink. "But it's wrong for a kid to be led into these ways, keeping all hours, getting up to no good with fellers—"

"Fellers?" Matthew echoed, "But they don't—?"

"Who knows? I don't. I don't say nothing."

"No, no," Matthew said, shaking his head and smiling. "She couldn't. Oh no."

Jacko's face hardened into its mask of a man-of-the-world, round the Cape seventeen times: "What is she made of then? Nut-cake?"

Across the room the chatter of voices was lessening. The bottle had run out. With less noise the room seemed to grow lighter, the smell of stale ash stronger. Only one voice droned on. One of the bearded men was upset by something, he stared with disgust at the girl in trousers and snarled: "Scampi, scampi, scampi— is the world made of *nothing* but scampi and poodles?

God above, I'd like to stuff all the poodles in the world
with all the scampi in the world and flush the lot down
the lou with a cistern of cappuccino. . . . "

"Why *is* it, Alfred, that you don't like things just because other people do?"

Alfred's beard shot back: his eyes widened: he splut-
tered: he looked like a man stabbed in the stomach
or faced with the truth.

And just then the door opened and Dawn came in
again with a woman in a close-fitting low-cut black
dress. Black as the night against white flesh, cut to
show crescents and ovals of sudden flesh, as if gloved
hands were already on it, the effect of the dress was
unequivocal; it made the woman in it a straight sexual
trap, a human pitcher-plant.

Ligne swore under his breath. It was the same girl
but seen as if through a distorting glass, reflected in a
dark mirror. Dead white now her face, and her eyes
heavily kohled against thick powder. A bitter purple
painted on her lips. Her hair drawn up, bound and
pulled, plaited above and back into a twisted crown,
and sprayed all over with a curious copper glint. A
black spot coquetted her cheek, and the shape of each
eye had been lengthened to give a long lid-dropping
look. Her breasts were pulled together to jut forward
and form a soft deep fissure, and more intimacies were
marked as, flowing away to show the flesh at her arm-
pits, the dark satin dress dropped near to her waist at
the back. A heavy perfume hung around her, gardenia,
thick and sickening.

A silence, a slight surprise in the air held their two

figures momentarily isolated—and on Matthew's mind there was photographed an intense memorable picture. The pink-haired Dawn, glittering with blue and silver sequins, a gross fantasy in pink and blue like a big coarse baby. And by her side this dark-clothed exotic plant, nightshaded, evil as a gilded little goddess in an eastern bar.

Dawn's metal-pink hair, curled and moulded hard like hair made of paint-sprayed pottery, shone in the shadow: her figure strutted rubber-stiff, her eyes were receded, lensed by the thick blue paint that lidded them—and as Matthew took all this in he began to feel a deep excited disgust, a loathing love for what had been done to the girl. A vulgarity pasted on with such efficient effect, as efficient as a pink silk shade, as successful as a crucifix on a whore's bosom. He hated what had happened—but whatever its quality, this painting and dressing-up had provided again the missing dimension, whatever he had missed when the girl had first come in, the complement of window-frame and dream.

"Because . . . because . . . BECAUSE!" the spluttering beardman suddenly exploded, "because it's not what people *like*, no it's because they like themselves liking what they like. Christ, how they *like* themselves!"

The girl's flat voice simply said: "And why shouldn't people like themselves?"

And Lily stepped forward to Matthew, swirled a little, and said: "And how do you like me?"

She said this quite innocently, no more than words to accompany entrance and expecting no answer.

Matthew could not stop himself: "How old are you?" he said, also expecting no answer.

"Why, twenty-one," Liliane smiled inside her mask, which also smiled above her smile.

"Then I don't like it," Matthew snapped.

A hand came on his elbow, Leslie's, and a whisper, "Steady on, old thing."

"You don't like me?" smiled Liliane over Lily. "But now Mr. Ligne, that's not altogether polite, is it?"

It was like talking to a girl within a girl; or somebody with a false nose on, or an actress heavily grease-painted in daylight off the film-set.

Dawn's eyes closed dangerously, moulding more blue. She sneered at him what must have ranked high in her invective: "Choosey, aren't you?"

"Yes, thank God," Ligne said.

"Oh? And what's so clever in being choosey then?"

Lily said: "Mr. Ligne only means he's at liberty to choose this or that, according to his lights. Don't you Mr. Ligne?"

"What the hell's it matter what Mr. Ligne thinks?" Dawn said. Even then, though she snapped this, she never moved her lips.

"I don't think it's at all funny," Ligne said coldly, "or clever, or amusing, for a girl of Lily's age to go to your nasty little club."

"Ay ay" muttered Leslie, "here we go—" as Dawn in her carefully clenched voice said: "I'm sure none of us will sleep at nights for what *Mister* Ligne thinks or doesn't think I don't think. Why shouldn't a girl have a bit of fun while she can?" she yelled.

"Fun?" Ligne echoed.

"Yes, fun, fun, FUN. You're the kind to put her behind a typewriter or a bloody counter, aren't you? You
don't mind her slaving away eight hours a day, week
after week, year after year, and not getting any
younger—it's nothing to *you*, is it? Well I'm going to
see she doesn't, see? I'm going to see she gets a bit of
fun while she can have it!"

Lily began: "Dawn, *please* . . . not here. . . . "

Dawn turned on her: "Well who the hell does he
think he is coming here and laying the law down?

Matthew said: "I'm very sorry. I was asked what I
thought. I gave my answer, that's all."

Lily, of everyone, seemed to remain unmoved. She
said quite soft, but sounding from within her make-up
like a calm young cobra: "You see Mr. Ligne, I've come
to live with my sister. It's very kind of her to have
introduced me into the—business, as it were. She thinks
it's a good idea, and I'm not sure I don't too. Life was
very slow where I came from in the country."

"Of course. It's no business of mine. I'm very sorry."

"In fact it was hellishly slow."

"Of course."

"So wouldn't you think it natural for me to enjoy the
bright lights a little?" She seemed to be discussing another person; already two selves, she introduced a
third. Matthew could only say: "Yes, yes of course. I
know." And add: "I know I'm keeping you now. So—
thanks—" he smiled equably at Dawn—"and goodnight."

He said this very suddenly and was out of the room

before any answer could be made. No one was sure whether this was rude or the best form of politeness. He left behind a bewildered small silence: in which only his footsteps sounded along the passage.

But they never descended the stairs. He abruptly changed his mind, and sensing where it would be, quietly opened the door to Lily's room. He switched on the light—and gazed at last on the long-yearned walls of his picture.

It was tremendously disappointing. It was just a room—four walls, wallpapers, bed, a dressing-table, chairs. A lamp that from the outside shone like a beacon was an ordinary lampshade on a stand. The mysterious wings of entry and exit to either side of the window were just quiet contained space, innocent, in a room. Instead of projected corners with no explanation, there were four ordinary walls.

But there was also the discovery of another reality—of the small realism of detail. Three objects stood out: a piece of underclothing lying across a chair; the photograph of a man in uniform on her dressing table; a book lying on the bedside table—a volume of Baudelaire, green and exact across the coloured cover of a woman's weekly magazine.

For perhaps the first time he thought. Who is she? The three objects, among so much else, among ornaments and mirrors and other clothes, formed a tripartite coat of arms: underclothing, photograph, book. Or, as his mind instantly confounded it—body, relationships, mind.

"Well?" she said behind him. "Enjoying yourself?"

He turned to the black and painted figure invading these thoughts of herself. And smiled. "I'm sorry, I took the wrong door."

"You do usually find doors on the staircase?"

"Oh, I don't know . . . new house. . . . " He was not prepared to be bothered by his patently false position. He had already involved himself pretty deeply by what he had said before. It was more important to ask: "I'd love to telephone you some time . . . may I?"

She seemed to accept this quite naturally. The youthful poise held. "Yes, do," she said.

"That's fine then. We could eat something."

"We could."

He felt very genial, as if much was settled: "Then I'll say goodnight."

"Goodnight."

He was out of the room, when she called after him: "But you don't know the number."

She even had to find a pencil to write it down for him.

EIGHT

HIS FINGERS, moving out to the telephone instrument, to the little black engine squatting and shining its inward smile—his fingers could now simply pick at numbers, swivel the dial, and cause her figure over in the room opposite to pause, listen, straighten up and stride away to unseen passages; there magically to become a voice loud in his room! The art, of course, lay in not doing this too often.

He remembered how, many years ago, when the newfangled telephone had first come to his parents' house, his mother had liked to telephone the lady exactly opposite across the street; and on a smiling morning these two ladies had sat in Japanese kimonos, kiss-curls flattened to the forehead in the style of the late post-war teens, and had talked for hours through the thin vulcanite, laughing and nodding across the street to each other as they spoke, heads even out of the window, as they enjoyed this wonder of science that enabled them, from the comfort of their bedrooms yet in full view of one another, to pursue their natural bent of putting thoughts into words.

He must not do that. In any case, he did not yet know her well enough. Telephoning must be limited to the making of appointments. There was a further difficulty. The first time he had tried, Dawn had answered. He did not immediately recognize her voice as she said: "Hallo, Yes, who wants her?" Hers was the voice with lips that never moved, and the very facelessness of the telephone failed to provide this important illusion. But when he did recognize it a second later—by ordinary defections of accent—he had already said his name, and she had replied that Lily was out. He should have made up a name: Amos Merryweather, John Strange, "tell her it's Dick."

The defect in Dawn's accent was very slight. However much Ligne disapproved his dislike of it, or even his labelling it a "defect"—his ear always reacted before his mind was brought to bear down fairly and classlessly. Dawn's were such little lapses. She pronounced "revolver" as "revo-o-lver," words like "ill" became "iwl," and she used "bought" for "brought" and "lay" for "lie" and so on. The very finest shade "off-colour." Yet why was there no such shade in Lily's voice? They were sisters. How had they been brought up, where with whom? What age was Dawn? A hundred such questions tickled at him as he waited, watching through the window, hand reaching for the telephone again.

"I'm pi-ining," pealed the Housewife, "foɪ the Argentine . . . " as she pinned up a long line of nappies. Beyond Mrs. Peabasin a dog whined, endlessly pathetic. From over the houses a pneumatic drill roared its spring song. Blackbirds sang from lilac now in blossom, and from nowhere there rose in a passing pocket of warm air the smell of roasting mutton. Two men in rain-coats had appeared in the laurel-garden where thoughts of murder dripped. They had their heads together in earnest discussion. Detectives, thought Ligne —at any minute they'll begin to dig.

Ligne sat and waited. He was becoming so practised that, though watching Miss Tigerpants standing before a mirror with an evening dress held up against her (What's that for? Ten to one a Barbecue!) he knew immediately from the corner of his eye, faceted now as a fly's, that Lily was back. The moment he saw her he telephoned. (Get her while's she's on her feet, she'll be the first to answer.) She did answer. And calmly, without prevarication of any kind, she accepted his proposal for a drink that evening, and rang off. This interchange was so short, so affirmative, so normal that he sat back shocked. He had imagined a hundred awkward pauses, stutterings, circumlocutions of every kind, blushes of the voice. But no. He might have been ordering fish.

He backed in from the window in case she looked over when she returned. She did. Quite casually, while arranging something or other in the room, she looked over. But since he was invisible, she simply went on doing what she was doing. He watched breathless. It seemed impossibly familiar of her, embarrassingly intimate. But he knew, and it made him the more uncomfortable, that she was simply being pleasantly natural. An accomplishment denied to himself.

"So you've spent all these years down in Flint, Miss McGhee?"

"Lily."

"Well, yes, Lily."

"Sorry, Liliane."

"Mm. Liliane."

They were sitting at one of the iron tables on the pavement outside a nearby saloon bar. Above a striped orange and green awning gave to the dung-grey London scene a dash of cordially bottled sunshine. Yet it was in fact a warm and sunny evening, bringing from the dust a goldish glitter of false summer; and overhead a cloudless blue sky threw chimney pots and high roofs into startling clear prominence.

"It's not as though the country was like the country any more," Liliane said. "If you see what I mean."

"No."

"People aren't bottling fruit and living in big families and piling old linen with lavender so much, you know."

"No, I don't suppose they are."

"They're whistling about in little cars and keeping in the swim. To and from the town, you know—the pictures, shopping, tins, you know."

"Yes."

"The country's getting provincial."

"I see what you mean."

"It's not the kind of swim I like. In any case with father dying that was really that, no point in staying, no money either. I didn't want to be a market gardener, did I?"

"No, you didn't."

"Can you see me keeping chickens?"

"Good Heavens no."

"So I came to live with Dawn and Dawn said why not have a shot at this Acacia Room stunt."

"Mm."

"Oh come off it, you'd think it was a brothel the way you go on. It's a night spot and I'm a country girl and I like it. It's only natural. After all these years. And you know in a way I'm in Dawn's hands, I've got to listen to what she says, I can't exactly live off her."

"But there are hundreds of other jobs."

"Do you know what they pay girls these enlightened days?"

"Of course you've got to start on not so much."

"I'd like that, wouldn't I?"

"Well why not for goodness sake? Everyone's got to begin."

"How long is it since you've been broke, or haven't you been?"

When he looked at her, it was her coolness that most astonished him. Young skins look cool; almost clammy. Yet this coolness went much further than textures—she had an absolute coolness of posture and eye and voice. Against the weathered daily background of brick and dust and older people passing she seemed to sit wrapped in an air of her own making, a cool cocoon. When her fingers touched her drink—he felt that a light, infinitely refreshing frost might bloom on the glass.

And the unflurried, concentrated, youthful gaze of her eyes. Older eyes, shifty with both sides of every question, tremble and start and look away: but youth concentrates, intent on accepting and rejecting. And so this girl concentrated and stared, and in any case he was prepared to be nervous, and such cool concentration, the opposite to indifference, made him the more so. But it tempted him too, and he ventured: "Obviously you're simply frightened of your elder sister. She's a forceful personality and you follow."

"True," was all she said.

There was little one could reply to this. He chose to make a big wince with his shoulders as two cars squealed high to a halt at a road-crossing opposite. This occurred at minute intervals. Sometimes bonnets nearly touched—and such near misses stimulated the drinkers thereabouts. Now Matthew managed to combine his shudder with a reproachful look at the girl.

"You're so utterly different from your sister," he said.

"We've had such utterly different lives."

Another pause. He began again:

"She was once—in the theatre, wasn't she?"

"Music Hall. Cabaret a bit."

"Why did she leave it then?"

"For the same reason she took it up. She can't stop at one thing alone. Likes a change. Oh I know you all think she's gone down-hill and all that, everybody does, but I wonder—she's seen a lot and done a lot, she's *alive*. . . ."

"But what *kind* of a life!"

He felt again: They're sisters and I've gone too far. But she only shook her head at the traffic, and went on: "Dawn gets things done, you know. She missed the kind of schooling I had—but's she's practical. I'm not.

It's a solution to follow her. Look how she left home—
no vacillation, *she* made a decision and *she* got her
traps together and set out. Nobody did it for her. I was
very much younger then and away at boarding-school
half the time—she wasn't deserting the ship or anything. The rest of us lived on at Stranraer—that was
the name of our awful red-brick house—my father and
Mrs. Haddy who kept house and I. Comfortable
enough. *Awfully* comfortable. Heavens, there were
three fir-trees in our garden: do you know how fed up,
how utterly fed up you can get with three tall fir-trees?
And a church tower, quite a nice church tower too. Oh
that *tower*."

Two more cars squealed to a halt and now it was
she who shuddered. In his mind's eye he saw a different village from the one she had described, and hated
it for her: it was a village where one day years ago he
had stopped for an hour's breakdown of his motor-car
—it had a church tower—and whenever he thought of
village and boredom the picture of this one erected
itself. But while he reproached this innocent substitute on her behalf, he was also thinking: she said
"vacillate." She did not say "shilly-shally" or anything.
She used "vacillate."

He realized he was watching her again—as surely as
if she had been at her window. And quite as surely
trying to erect round her real presence the old mystery, the extra dimension. But now from the inside. She
was a person with a personality, no more now the cut-
out figure of a girl he had for the past month from a
mindless distance worshipped: she had a quick to be

got at. How many of the silent gods and goddesses we admire on the street and in passing vehicles, those who catch at our throats and perhaps remain forever in memory as images ideal—how many would remain so if we met and talked with them? Out from the mystery comes the same old pattern, pattern of words and pattern of moving face, and it is all over . . . unless. . . . But why should the presence of any one particular person prove so delightful? So pleasing that years rise off the shoulders? For no good reason he could easily find. The place was swimming with young and pretty girls. There were as good fish in the sea. Then why this one? It couldn't be, Matthew thought, because she seems so interested in you, you old horror, and hangs on your eyes?

"No," she was saying, "I've never been out of England. So, if you come to think of it, London is kind of out of England for me. It's a parallel."

A "parallel" she had said. Three syllables, he noted. And had he been talking about this new café-table-outside atmosphere in London? As if he had spoken days ago, he recalled words said a minute before and went on: "Could we then be somewhere or other abroad? Table, pavement, parasol. Blue sky, even a plane-tree—not in leaf yet, but that dappled bark gives us a feeling of dappled sunshine, hein? A *gay* little *bistro* on the Mediterranean?"

"The tide's out," she said looking at the empty tarmac broadening over the street.

"Not the Mediterranean, then. Yet—" and he pointed across the road to where a milk station showed through open doors its raised quays: the little whirring orange

floats whined in and out, electric smacks taking on
cargoes of bottles from the cobbled quays, "—yet there
seems to be a harbour."

Two youths passed by on cycles, one shouting: "I'll
——ing well do you, you——ing bastard!"

"Of course, there's the language difficulty," Lily said.

"On a clear day," Matthew whispered, pointing to a
pavemented traffic sign in the middle of the road, "you
can see the island."

And on they went, the two of them, the near-forty
and twenty-one, playing at cafés. He suddenly realized
that he was in fact "playing"—"having fun." It had not
happened in years.

What had occurred? He felt frightened that the
moment might pass and he went in to get two further
drinks, there being no waiters in this café. Nor were
there saucers, nor ashtrays, nor table-wiping—in fact
they sat among grime drinking off virulent green paint.
And the passers-by stared at them rather than vice
versa. But otherwise it was good, there was the passing
street and the blue sky and the excitant taste of drink
drunk outside among stale, petrol-sweet breezes.
Matthew bought two enormous glasses of absinth, forgetting that the noisome old liquorice-milk probably
meant nothing to Lily-Liliane.

He was certainly feeling very good: no trace of his
ulcer. It was noticeable that this disappeared not always when wanted but often when true euphoria rose
in him. And he seemed to have risen above self-
criticism; normally he might have noticed that he had
criticized Dawn for forcing a similarly large drink on

the girl the night before; now, how innocent this seemed!

He found, too, that he took a simple delight in pointing out to her one or two local colours: old Sir Hugh buzzing along the neighbouring street erect on his mini-motorcycle, bare knees clenched at putt-a-putt-a-putt speed, shoulders bent intent on the urgency of his errand; that young matron Margot walking the pram by their very table without noticing—with the angry little Mongolian blossomed in a month to a stern crop-headed Hindenburg figure—and he was simply delighted to sit and watch her pass, and then recount the little episode of "demand feeding" on the party night. He felt no embarrassment. He even told her he was watching from the little coat-clustered upper room. "At least that's one night you weren't out at your beastly Acacia place," he ended suddenly bitterly. Then laughed to cover it. But she began defending the job again: "And another thing—we're free during the day. Think how many Londoners working in an office never have time to go out and see a thing all their lives—it's an old story."

Sitting up there so self-contained, talking about "old stories," he thought. How can youth *know* about these "old stories"?

"But then," she continued, "if you're out looking at things and work at night, there's no time to read. And possibly people read more quietly after dark? I never really know. On the other hand aren't we supposed to be night-monkeys, or something, and wake up at the change to dark?"

"Possibly," he said wondering. "But in any case, it's rather better to be awake when you've a book in your hands, isn't it? Do you read much yourself?"

"Heavens, yes. That is, within reason."

Heavens above, he thought, there we go again: "Within reason." But why not? Twenty-one was quite an age. Or was it parrot-talk?

He found out that she did in fact read Baudelaire but found him rather "old hat," which was natural in her opinion, since he was an innovator and a master . . . and as gradually he learned more of her situation and ideas—he discovered that the photograph of the young man in an officer's cap was after all only her father taken during the Kaiser's War. A fact which he first welcomed as eliminating a possible rival, and the next moment deplored, as it might mean she was a daddy's-girl, a fact which might explain her coolness as coldness and involve a much more formidable rivalry —and as they sat talking he simply went on thinking, beyond everything, beyond all practical informations, who is she, who *is* she?

Which one may spend a lifetime thinking, with always the face and never the answer. And he sat observing her with what felt a most inapposite clarity. For, if this was love, should he not be wearing rose-coloured glasses, should he not be heady, glazed, blinded? He was certainly not blind. He still had the feeling of having looked at her first in a mirror, and now of turning to see the real, less magical image. Perhaps what he now looked at, with its posing of questions greater than mere appearance, he saw with too forced a clarity and concentration, fabricating thus a deeper illusion, seeing too clearly and too much.

Perhaps this is the kind of illusion love breeds? Or perhaps it's the absinth. He looked down at his glass. Absinth is known to produce a different kind of intoxication. Broadens the mind. But does it? Perhaps it only opens the mind, so that you simply see and feel *more* things, not more things more clearly. (His eye left the glass and took in the London Street—and he saw immediately and clearly that with the ingredients of café-table, sun-blind, plane-tree, blue sky, new white paint and a jumble of red Edwardian buildings that might have been Belgian as much as English, he saw that the absolute factor that made this England and nowhere else was the pavement, the kerb and the road surface. Nowhere else were there paving stones and kerb exactly like these: and this large surface beneath our feet, and beneath where we like to think our eyes look, was decisive?)

Well, the old absinth made him see these lower surfaces of truth very clearly, and, it seemed, suddenly. But was it the absinth—he had not drunk more than a glass? Or was it some unique excitement this girl contrived?

They rose to go. He asked her whether they might meet next day, have lunch together? She agreed instantly. Again no prevarication, no difficulty—simple and easy gracious acceptance. Things were going exactly right. This gave him an instant feeling that something was wrong. He was immediately, in a superstitious sense, suspicious.

Nevertheless, as she went off—as he well knew soon to dress and go on show at the nefarious Acacia Room —he was so curiously excited he could not feel properly downcast.

Strolling home, he was accosted by a small boy. For a few seconds conversation was unintelligible—the boy wore over his head a transparent space-helmet. When this was raised, Matthew received no enquiry for the right time or whatever else might be expected, but instead:

"Do you like even or odd numbers?"

For a moment he was too surprised to answer. Then the boy whispered: "Say you like evens. I do."

And back through the long years he remembered this old game of dividing life into right hands and left hands, positives and negatives. His own tendency was to the left, to the odds. But now he found himself easily and happily confirming to the small boy:

"Evens. Every time."

The boy clapped his hands and said: "Do you like lions best or tigers?"

"Lions!" Matthew said. He replaced the boy's space-helmet, and walked on feeling as if he had effected something very simple and affirmative, like saying his prayers and meaning them; reconciled for a moment with the world, lighter-hearted for the pillow-sweet sound of humanity's favourite word, yes.

Then the boy toddled after him, raised the helmet himself, and said: "Isn't it funny—I think of seven like an even number. Only it isn't, is it? Not really?"

So it was not so simple after all.

◆

NINE

◆

AFTER THE RISE, a let-down: euphoria took its toll, the
scales of emotional justice weighed down on him, and
he sat at his window with less easy, more uncertain
thoughts than ever.

The week was brilliant. He met Lily-Liliane several
times, and at each meeting liked her more than the last.
And she seemed to enjoy him, too. It was all too disconcerting, it couldn't last. Nothing was wrong, so he
thought everything was. He felt like a man on runaway skates, trembling for the fall, fabricating the fall.

That is why, after a week, against half his will and
all his better judgment, he buttoned on a clean shirt to
pay a surprise visit to the Acacia Room. But these
buttons did not enter their holes easily, one at least
came undone when already fastened—it seemed as
though one hand were doing them up and the other
bent on undoing all that had been done.

He knew that seeing her in this club would anger
him—and that this might lead to some outburst: but he
was damned if she should lead this public private life
to his exclusion! He wanted to face up to things, not

avoid them. And he wanted to see her once more in that astonishing painted travesty—would she act differently? He wanted to see whether he would feel estranged by this appearance, even disgusted. He wanted to prove to himself that escape from her was finally impossible: or to formulate that escape altogether.

They had met on the day following their first drink in the pub, and had lunched not in the old and well-brassed restaurant he had chosen, but—on her suggestion—in a new vegetarian restaurant. For fun! Nut cutlets (Our own Nutlets), prime ribs of celery, and a jocose pudding called Never-say-Pie. "If you don't do these things," she argued, "you'll never know what they're like." "Like being crucified?" he asked. They had enjoyed themselves immensely, and agreed never to go again.

Afterwards he had found himself covered with pigeons in Trafalgar Square. Then he endured an hour on the Inner Circle Underground, popping up at this or that station to sniff the district (he calmed an initial disquiet by remembering he had always wanted to do the same with the Paris Metro—those names!). He had wandered up the Bloody Tower; and been surprised by the magnificence of the changing of the Palace guard. They had looked at early wax aviators in South Kensington, a bitterly cold Chinaman in Limehouse, gaslit porters at Covent Garden (6 a. m.). They had visited Oscar Wilde's platform at Clapham Junction, and sat for over an hour in Harrod's Bank. Finally she had enjoined him to what she called a "liquid lunch," a pub-crawl between the outlying inns on Hampstead

Heath: it had been a wild May day, high with rain-showers, blowing with blossom—and he had exorcised two further of his minor dislikes, beer and mackintoshes. He wondered about that "liquid lunch"—such heartiness occasionally salted her talk. He blamed whatever young men there had been to hand in her home village. Blamed? "And why not?" he was endeared to rebuke himself.

So they had had fun. It was plain that they were mutually stimulated. But he was still suspicious. Exactly on what basis did he come into her life? He was nearly twenty years older than she was. Did she think of him as a kind of jolly uncle? Within her high spirits he detected a kind of coolness. Was this just the cool look, the pure look, of youth? And he was not yet prepared to spoil this by suggesting anything too much—the moment was even too precious to risk a kiss: they sometimes walked with arms linked—a friendly gesture, but to him embarrassingly intimate. Once he almost kissed her—but stopped himself just in time. It might spoil everything. It was debased coinage. This little discipline made him feel again the delightfully pure and exultant sensations of boyhood.

And he wondered—where, for instance, were the young men of her own age? It was absurd that someone had not somehow sought her out. Perhaps she didn't like young men? Did that make him some kind of a substitute for daddy-love? And then he thought: Perhaps the attentions of the gentlemen at the Acacia provided her with a surfeit—he refused to think to what degree—and was he a foil for this?

There was another matter that he found particularly disconcerting. The whole relationship affected his customary life at the window. Now that he knew her so well, it became embarrassing to look across. In the first place it might look like spying; in the second he might catch her eye—and then there would be a wordless mouthing and waving with neither knowing how to end it, for the first to withdraw would appear rude. It would be like recognizing someone from afar in a theatre when the lights go up—how, once begun, to stop smiling and nodding, where next to look?

He prayed, too, that she would never undress without drawing the curtains. He imagined his criminal guilt, drawn to watch against all good intention, and winced. Then he thought of Leslie and shuddered.

So he made even greater efforts to efface his presence from this window to which he was spiritually wedded. He moved his chair half behind a curtain fold, arranged a permanent book propped ready for absorbed attention, and on even quite chilly days raised the window sash so that two lateral white bars came close together to form an elementary screen, through whose interstices he would self-consciously glance across without feeling he was seen. But he took even greater pains to keep himself well-brushed and dressed in case she should see him—even once to the extent of a silk dressing-gown and scarf.

He found it hard to believe that life in the gardens could go on in ignorance of these tensions. Miss Tigerpants and her poodle still played the oblivious scene of their lives at the window—Miss Tigerpants was teaching her Poo tricks, so that one saw Miss Tiger-pants kneeling with her paws begging on the carpet and the poodle watching her from the table, uneasy and embarrassed. The sober and well-kempt couple next door still walked forward to bend crescent stout-nesses to the paving for a forbidden twig, a blown laburnum spray. Smells of cooking still rose and van-ished fitfully, telling of personal meals consumed privately in rooms unknown. Mrs. Peabasin still pot-tered her cottage round, and her garden with the growth of May grew greener: now she had hung it with scraps of bright tin-foil to scare the birds—in fact frightening the neighbours, who caught sudden flashes in the corner of the eye. The laurel garden below to the right bloomed dismally with the new slight life of those two men in rain-coats, who appeared, chatted, smoked and disappeared. The man who carried his bicycle so dutifully upstairs each night to the landing was, of course, now identified as Jacko: this, and a sudden quiet over the Average Housewife's garden, the result probably of an early "staggered" family holiday, were the only changes to be observed.

But much more was changing, slowly, just per-ceptibly. Rogue seeds had arrived from over the roof-tops, growing into stout-bearded weeds and trees; and insects of all kinds were stirring for the summer rout. But such developments were so slow: he wanted some-thing sharp and disruptive to happen—something to match his own yearning for action. Thus, in the minia-ture landscape below, he now treasured any small revolution. A morning of frost, when the gardens went

mad with seagulls playing the pigeon. He longed for
July when the ants rose, and hundreds of them enlivened with short ecstasy the window-panes; for
hover-flies in high summer, pretty little helicopters
jerseyed in yellow and black, standing all about the
air on their wings; or spiders drifting in on a single
silver thread, mariners of the day air; or a windy day
with the air wild with parachute seed. But just now
how slowly the spring swelled to burst, how slow the
fattening of sun-hungry leaf and fly-crazy flower raising
their new architecture of green within and above the
garden walls—giant beans gathering force, trees describing the summer shade, but all slow, so slow—

When suddenly, impatient of all this, Matthew
realized for the first time her window would soon disappear altogether! A filigree of plane-branches, now
bobbled with ball-seed like a Spanish veil, would soon
stretch their starfish leaves right across her window!
There was a time limit! His anxieties redoubled. To be
able to watch her was distressing, but to be unable far
worse.

Does one recall those times in childhood when a
prized and wonderful possession was loved? A shining
tricycle, a doll with real hair and a silken dress that
must be looked at just once more before going to bed?
How treasured their images later in the dark: "I
mustn't—I *mustn't* go to sleep. I mustn't waste a think."
It was in just such a way that Matthew's private mind
dwelled on this Lily-Liliane's face, bringing it again and
again alive in his imagination, tasting it with his mind's
eye, listening to what it said, watching how it moved.

Sometimes he could glance over the gardens and see her profile, and then he tried to reconstruct her reality from this distant puppet. The two were difficult to reconcile. But the binoculars? He was now too involved to use them. However—no shame held his mind as it held the hand at the binoculars: in his mind he could not be found out, and simply since no one could see his thoughts, he went on thinking.

Her straight back-brushed fair hair so highly crowned and the dark contrast of red-brown not blue eyes never ceased to be unexpected: the firm chin, with its long and grave upper lip, was a further mystery—this again provoked some kind of question that he wanted to bite into for an answer. She was left-handed, and sometimes this gave her a slightly crippled look: it invited help. He looked for defects—this a little large, and that a little long or small—, found them, and could not dislike them. And he could see quite clearly the greatest defect of all—that another man might not find her at all unusual. But that kind of knowledge naturally did nothing to disillusion him.

He sat watching Miss Tigerpants change her brassière and wondered about that "liquid lunch," or adolescences like "pessimist" and "dubious," or a smart "chums" for "friends" or "ball" for "party" and how he felt affection where otherwise he would have flinched. He marvelled at her quick changes of emotion, one moment pensive, the next bright with laughter. The young look hungry, he thought as though they might bite. Sudden lapses of taste were enchanting, sudden gaps of knowledge disarming. Only one kind of gap shocked him—an ignorance of what was going on even ten years before, a very real reminder of the difference between their ages. He brooded on this. He brooded on the possibilty of his being a father figure to her. He wondered also whether that boyishness about her had stimulated a latent homosexuality in him. He decided that neither mattered. Life was far to diverse to worry about such deep resources. Meanwhile his ulcer seemed to have cured itself. His monograph had lost all its appeal. He wished only for action. Yet he had never seriously wondered—what am I going to do about all this? He was still stunned. But that itch for action, like a blind grub nosing into life, had begun.

The daily round continued. Leslie, Mrs. Orme and Sir Hugh continued—they were on the stairs and about his rooms as usual, their presence demanding. Only Mrs. Orme remained truly inexpendible. Sir Hugh's purpose in calling at all—to "get the young fellow out of himself"—had plainly ceased to be necessary. But one day Leslie happened to bring home a second-hand tape recorder to be sold on a commission basis. Seeing it, Ligne saw the light. He showed it to Sir Hugh. The old man was delighted. His bald old baby's face sniffed the intricate grey metal as it should have sniffed a buttonhole of violets.

"Then it's yours, Uncle," Matthew said. "You can make reel after reel about the divine Buggé and the gay chapkas of the Lancers jingling in the morning sunlight—"

"Lot of square bashing in public," the old man began to grumble. "Cost a lot of time and money and held up the traffic. . . . " But the magic worked. The little grey mouthpiece sucked long forgotten marrow from the old man's bones and provided Matthew with a book he no longer wanted to write.

But Leslie remained mournfully on the premises. Waiting to wait on an invalid who was hardly ever there. Matthew had not the heart to turn him out, which one day he must do. Even the old game they used to play with the people in the gardens had to be avoided now.

It was a difficult, bewildering time.

So, a little after eleven o'clock in the evening of a particularly frustrating day, he went out to search with a worried heart for the Acacia Room.

The taxi-driver drove him without comment—as if he had been driving Matthew there every night of the year: again that awful indifference of life continuing. Matthew's impulse was to stroll a little before going in: but he detected cowardice and had already passed through the vestibule before being called back to pay his subscription and entrance fee.

From inside a thudding, as if some muffled old beam engine were at work, told that the music had begun. Fearful to be discovered and possibly barred by Dawn, he floundered the money into the hands of an arrogant moustached man with a military tie, wrote his name a couple of times and hurried on in, holding his head bent to one side in an attempt to hide himself.

He saw Lily immediately. Her back was turned, a

low chairback hid the even lower back of her dress and she might have been naked but for the piled hairdress, which gave her in fact an over-decorated effect. She sat with Dawn, two other girls, and a man in a black tie, probably a head waiter. Matthew made for the opposite end of the empty room.

A small dark waiter with frightened eyes, filthy black trousers and a brilliantly white coat showed him to a spotless table and brought him a bottle and some soda water.

White table-cloths shone in patches all over the room to the discomfort of walls and floor, which needed a coat of paint and a new carpet. The whole place had the battered, paint-chipped look of a fairground booth. Acacia leaves painted on the walls had lost their branches and looked like spots of old green confetti, an attempt had been made with scarlet paint to outline and freshen up doors and the wood surrounds of banquettes, whose threadbare aquamarine plush was not dark enough to hide the long absorption of drinks, food and possibly worse that stained it. Chianti bottles were strung on the walls among fishing nets and painted plaster masks, and there were more chianti bottles on the tables with dust-smeared red candle-grease dribbled down their sides. It was indeed chianti-land, not quite in Mayfair, and the whole room smelled of stale biscuits, the result of a fusion of scent, sweat and fried food.

The band sat in a little house made of pink bamboo stalk roofed with a tattering of grime-soaked raffia.

They were mostly smooth serious men, two of whom wore rimless octagonal spectacles and clipped blond moustache-lines: there was also a negroid drummer the colour of a soaked cigarette, and a sad white-faced pianist. The leader, strong and oiled and levantine, dispensed his music with the fat smile of a rich man over-tipping. He tipped Matthew a smile as he sat down.

Dawn saw him instantly, and Lily seeing Dawn's expression, turned.

She came straight over. She was not smiling. All his built-up irritation sank away, he felt guilty as a school-boy found out.

"Hello," she said, "this *is* a surprise!"

"I thought I'd drop in," he said to the white powder, the black kohl, the purple lips larger than her own. He peered for the face behind all this, searching for sympathy.

"It's a bit early," she said. "We're empty. Not very amusing for you I'm afraid."

"Well of course I didn't come to be—" He stopped.

She caught it instantly: "To be amused? Then what did you come for?"

"To see you, of course," he appealed.

They were both standing. It was absurdly formal after their usual intimacy. He added: "Let's sit down, won't you?"

"I shall have to go," she said, sitting but still un-smiling. "So you came to see me? Why didn't you tele-phone?"

"Why will you have to go?" he asked.

"Why?" She picked at a finger-nail. New-laid varnish flaked off. "Damn," she said. "Oh, a party telephoned. A regular."

"Oh."

"Well now you're here, what d'you think of it?"

"A man?"

"Heavens no. A dear old lady. In a lace cap."

"You're very funny."

She turned at him impatiently. "Well what do you expect coming here like this? I know you don't approve. You never stop going out of your way to say so. If ever it's mentioned you pull a long face. And now you arrive calm as a coot and say you've come to see *me*. You know you can see me any time."

He was so frightened he began to lie: "But I was at a loose end, I just thought I'd—"

"Loose end nothing," she said. "You're at a loose end most of the time and you know it. And you didn't come to see me at all, you came to see me *here*, which is quite a different thing."

"Yes," he said lamely, "yes."

"In fact you came to spy. Nothing less."

Spy, like lie, is a ruffling word. Matthew's voice rose: "You don't understand," he said, "you don't understand!"

"Understand what?"

He paused, wondering what. The room was peppering with newly arrived guests. "That I came possibly to hurt myself," he murmured, "and that I did so want to see you, really I want to know everything about you. . . ."

During the whole time they had spent together, he had never made so personal an affirmation.

She put her hand on his and nodded. It might have looked as if she were taking his pulse. "I see," she said "Sorry."

The words he had spoken freed others: "I do adore you so," he mumbled, looking down at their two hands, as if this were something shameful to say.

She said quite clearly. "And I do too." Then added softer: "But not here—"

Out of the mouth of the saxophones curled the melody of that ubiquitous Argentine song, and this with its echo of the gardens made him see her more clearly as up at her window than here in travesty and so he said: "No, you're right. But this one evening, can't you put off this—"

He was not sure what awful word to use—"client"? "gentleman"?—and paused, and then a voice above them said: "Hello! Slumming?"

He looked up over sequined sapphire to see light little fangs appear, smile-recorders like ivory dimples to either side beneath eyes sparkling with trouble.

He managed to smile back. "Good evening, Miss McGhee."

"Alone?" she said.

"I just looked in."

"So does the Sanitary Inspector from time to time," she said, tasting him with her eyes like a bully, "he finds it okay."

"Now Miss McGhee—Dawn, can I say?" he smiled,

and risked: "I'm only the ratcatcher. Just called to see this little rat here."

"Well, your little rat's engaged to work here—Mr. *Ligne,* can I say?"

"I imagined my money was as good as anyone else's," he smiled, and gestured pleasantly at his bottle: "Won't you in any case," he rose now, "sit down had have one?"

It was difficult to bully a smile. And the mention of money clicked him mechanically into a different register. Something tense about her arms slackened: "You don't seem to be getting on with it too well, yourself," she said pointing at the bottle.

"I know, it's my confounded stomach," he said. This was true. Once again this evening he had felt a premonitory twinge: it meant trouble later on, he would have to go easy. The alternative method of paralysing the thing with too much liquor was too dangerous to try often.

But this gave Dawn the chance of a disguised kidney-punch. She sat down and said delightedly: "We can't have that in the Acacia! Now you just take a good old swig to please me."

"No, really," he began. But she filled all the glasses, laughing gaily and knowing exactly what she was doing.

All this time Lily had said nothing. Matthew imagined that this was Dawn's domination—when suddenly she spoke, and calmly with authority: "Come on, I can't bear this squabbling. Have a drink, Dawn. You needn't if you don't want to, Matthew."

She sighed and added: "Let's have a moment's peace before my Mr. Sanderson comes."

She looked immeasurably tired behind her white face. How often though, the young look pale and tired, whacked, he said to himself. However whacked or not, they were always ready to stay up, go on, never, *never* stop . . . , whereas he, approaching forty?

He took a sip of his drink to please Mother McGhee. They all sighed more amicably. "That's better." But it was not better. His head knocked with the remembrance of Lily saying—"I do too." All he wanted was to get away and think about it. His head began to ache, and he smiled the more broadly.

Several couples were dancing. The lights were low. Shadow and light clouded the floor in something not a mist nor darkness—a kind of shadowed inexactitude. Only the pale-eyed faces of the band showed certain and bright—they pored like a row of chemists dispensing above the little lights hidden in their music stands. A livelier tune was playing, something from Brazil, and through the growing tinkle of glass and the fog of voices and tobacco smoke, the negro drummer his constantly at a hollow gourd that clacked like a hammer inside Matthew's own skull.

Nevertheless since he thoroughly disliked and despised Dawn he found it curiously easy to be pleasant: in fact to be thoroughly false. She laughed and joked heavily; but the suspicion and dislike never left her eyes, she was on edge and he felt that the slighest mistake would start her. Lily knew this too, and perhaps said little only to keep the peace: Such quiet had the effect of increasing the withdrawn quality that in any case made such mystery for Matthew.

Then Dawn saw a middle-aged man, a man in a well-filled business-man's suit and wearing dark-rimmed glasses, stand for a moment in the entrance. She was delighted to lean across and shout to Lily: "There's Sanderson!"

"So it is," Lily said.

She looked for a moment helplessly down at the ash-smeared table-cloth. She pushed her finger over the ash, smearing it further. All the poise had gone. Matthew saw immediately how embarrassing it was, and wished to heaven he had not come.

"You'd better get going then," Dawn said.

"Yes," she said quietly, thanked Matthew without looking at him, rose and left.

She looked downcast as a child. But he saw her straighten as she crossed the room. He cursed himself; but he stayed, tormented curiosity held him. What he had expected he did not know but he felt an absurd relief when the man smiled pleasantly at her and they shook hands. Yet a moment later, as the man guided her to a table, his hand was touching her elbow. The little gesture looked enormously possessive.

Dawn was saying: "You think she's too young for this job don't you!" She drawled it, still smiling, lingering on the edge of her words.

He pretended to yawn: "Yes. Well. Yes, I suppose I do."

"Then," Dawn leaned closer, "that means she's too

young for you, too, doesn't it? Doesn't *that* occur to you?"

He held on to himself hard. The music seemed to blare louder. "I don't know," he said casually, "besides, the two things are rather different."

"How? You're about twice her age, aren't you?"

He had to pull her up. His mind sought wildly and landed with a bump on what astonished him: "Everyone knows there are many happy marriages despite such discrepancies of age."

His eyebrows raised themselves as his own ears heard these words. Dawn made a throttled sound: "*What?*"

Then: "*What* marriage? You and her?"

He managed to say quite quietly: "I was only speaking objectively."

"What's that mean?"

"It means, dispassionately. You know, involving none present. Present company excepted."

"Passion? What are you talking about? What's it but bloody baby-snatching? That's what you are, a bloody—"

Before she had finished he was on his feet, angry, but his own words still hammering wonder in his ears: "Come on, let's dance," he laughed.

Dawn was so surprised she let him take her jogging into the bodies on the floor. "Well I must say," she said.

But dancing was automatic with her, it was not the gesture of truce it seemed. She was put out, exasperated and dangerous. He could sense a tenseness in her body like an animal bunching its muscles—but was this no more than stoutness, corsetry?

Whatever, it was a secondary consideration. As they shuffled round miraculously untouching among the other dark couples, Matthew's mind still hammered amazement at what he had said, amazement at the idea of marriage, amazement at not thinking of it before. Was it unnatural for him to think what others thought naturally? And in all the vague confusion of half-darkness and music and movement and smoke and laughter, with such thoughts giant and conflicting in his mind—his eyes were still free to watch Lily every time he came round in view of her table. She was, it appeared, talking ordinarily and amicably with the man Sanderson. Occasionally, this man leaned forward towards her, laughing. This was not what Matthew had expected—he had steeled himself against he did not know what . . . amorous play of some sort, arms round shoulders or hands clasped—but this friendliness was finally the more disconcerting, simply because of an ease in the man's behaviour, as if he possessed her and thus felt no need to make advances: such was the effect of perfectly decorous, enjoyable behaviour! It upset Matthew so much that he steered himself away, preferring the risk of sitting down again with Dawn.

But as soon as they sat down Lily and Sanderson got up to dance. Sanderson must have been a young fifty, a well-filled man with a reddish face, plastered grey hair, owlish thick glasses; active on his feet,

polished and easy and successful. Matthew suddenly
saw him stripped to his underclothing—suspenders and
pants strutting about a bedroom, patting talcum powder on his big red chin: the red stopped at Sanderson's neck, beneath the collar-line his skin was white as
a grub. Suddenly he saw Sanderson's hand on Lily's
back. It was held away from the flesh, consciously
conniving with the bare back. He swallowed and
looked away.

Dawn seemed content to drink and grumble dis-
jointedly about people in the room. Once the man at
the reception desk, ginger whiskers and military tie,
came by, paused and laughed with a wink: "Hello!
Didn't know you knew Ma McGhee! Shocking type,
eh?" Matthew took the well-known cliché literally—
and felt a stronger distaste than ever for such a woman
in charge of Lily's future. "Lily and Dawn" he muttered
to himself, tasting horror into the names, "Good God!
Might as well be Lois and Belle." Lil, he thought.
Liliane. Lilian. But Lily—Lily was really very lovable
if you looked at it simply, no Dawn about. . . .

Two tables away sat another of the hostesses, a large
dark-haired girl who talked very loudly. Occasionally
Dawn half-turned and shuddered as this girl's voice
gusted across: "Christ!" she said, "that Estelle Pearson.
Vaccinated with a bloody gramophone needle." And a
moment later, a kind of grumbling growled louder in
her: "On the bash I shouldn't wonder. Fool to employ
her." She sat there stoking up all her temper against
this Estelle. Matthew let her.

They got up to dance again and got jammed for a

while exactly opposite this Estelle's table. She was a big girl in a bright scarlet dress. Her skin was white and looked hard as rubber, her thick hair was oiled back to spread out fuzzing like a black peacock's fan eyed with little plastic combs and rings, and there was a strong feathered look about her dark-moustached upper lip above orange lipstick. Her voice came over louder. Whatever she said sounded like a cooking recipe, I-do-this, I-take-that, I-simmer-till-brown. Now it rose in strident reproach: "*I'm* not one to speak, not when I'm not asked, but *I* for one say she's what *I* call a . . . "

Dawn grated quietly by his shoulder: "What *I* call, what *I* call," and she was still muttering halfway round the room, fanning herself into a rage—and then they were past the gently bouncing figures of the band and back at Estelle's table again, and Estelle was still at it: "D'you know what I call it? I call it *not nice at all,* that's what I call it—" And Dawn suddenly shouted straight down into her face: "And why don't you shut what *you* call your mouth?"

The dark head jolted up, caught in mid-sentence, took it all in instantly, and chose to say coldly: "I *beg* your pardon?"

Dawn's hands went to her hips, her great pink chin stuck out like a fist. "You heard me," she drawled, licking the words, "I said, why don't you shut what you call your bleeding mouth?"

Estelle's large white bosom rose and fell quickly; there was an animal inside trying to get out: "I thought that was what you said," she cooed hard. Her black-ringed mascaraed eyes were thinned into slits; she sat

tensed and very upright; with eyes thus closed, anyone not knowing might have thought her fallen asleep
sitting up.

"Well shut it then!" Dawn spat.

The man with Estelle was saying: "I say, I say now
. . . " and Matthew had a hold on Dawn's arm, gently
pulling her, but this arm she snatched free as Estelle,
half-rising, her bosom bolting and a great breath
sucked in through lower teeth bared, snatched up the
nearest tumbler and tossed what was in it into Dawn's
face, who cried out "Oh!" and looked slowly down
blue sequins dribbling long dark stains of still bubbling
beer.

A hand went up to the dark girl's mouth as she realized what she had done. She looked terrified.

She wrenched herself sideways and up to make a
diving run for it. But Dawn blocked her—and then for
a momentous second they stood face to face, breathing
heavily, anger and fear blazing hard diamonds in their
eyes.

Both women now seemed to swell in their plumage
of silk and sequin and bangle and earring, like birds
strutting to the dance, faces screwed into war masks,
Estelle's mouth down-drawn oblong as a dragons-dog,
Dawn's set in a cruel crescent, both showing pink
within the painted lip-rouge, both widening and
straightening backs and arching necks like great cats
raising a scruff . . . and filled with a great intake of
breath they stayed for a moment poised, the pink-
haired and the dark, two big dangerous women.

Men never went through so rich an address; it was

savagely formal, like the old brazen picture of prosti-
tutes brawling—when first, breathing hard, eyes coldly
interlanced, both ladies would remove from their heads
their huge feathered hats, taking their time, pulling out
each pin, placing them carefully on the kerb—and only
then rising to fly screaming at each other, tearing tooth
and nail.

No words more—a sudden high wail from all her
throat as Dawn thrashed out a fat pink arm and
grabbed at the top of Estelle's thick black hair, pulling
her down and through the tables to skitter with hands
out and grunt blindly, tears of hairpain and rage cloud-
ing eyes—then to twist round and up with teeth into
Dawn's forearm, so that Dawn snatched away and
brought long lacquered nails like blunted razors across
the girl's shoulder. Then they were hitting, biting, kicking, scratching all round and over, no sound but grunt
and breath of effort, bending and swaying, the red
dress and the blue, the black hair and the pink like
wild exotic dancers in dreadful ecstasy—before the men
were at them to pull them flailing apart, it needed two
men to each woman, and Estelle's hand at the last
moment grabbed up a short bright fork from the table—
and with this made a vicious stabbing gesture as the
man with a military tie took up a siphon of soda, and,
it seemed quite casually, drenched her with it.

Wetness is sudden, shocking—it sobered her into
words and at the top of her scream yelled long abuse at
Dawn who flung it back higher, noise and language
tore the air open and the band played louder to drown

it and Estelle was frogmarched kicking and scratching away somewhere outside.

Matthew was still holding Dawn. He looked down astonished at her dress—neither woman had torn or grasped the other's clothes: something sacred? Now suddenly her whole strength seemed to give, she looked more a woman than Matthew had ever seen her, as, sitting down bowed and small, she broke into tears.

One eye was closed, she was covered with lager—he saw her pink disordered hair was flecked with yellow-grey roots and there were red nail-marks on her arms and cheek. Lily was over and had her arm round her, not cooing condolence but repeating sharply: "Come on. Snap out of it. We're going home." Again and again, cool and certain as a nurse, until she got the message through and had her up by the arm and straight through the dancers to the door.

They disappeared, several people laughed, and Matthew saw with surprise that the man who had held Dawn's other arm was Sanderson. "That," said Sanderson to him, as if they were old friends, "has put the kibosh on that."

"On what?"

"On my little evening."

"Oh."

"Come and have a drink."

There seemed to be no reason to refuse.

He went over with Sanderson and sat down where Lily had sat. He looked at her half-finished haddock. "Her haddock," he thought. But then looked away—

he was intruding, staring at where her intimate fork had been it was in some slight way almost like peeking at her half-undressed in a window. Little boxes of book-matches crumpled on the table, a cigarette-end in the ashtray with its purple ring of lip rouge, ash smeared on the white cloth, stale glasses of whiskey and soda—it all had a used look. Despite a gnawing pain in his stomach Matthew took the drink offered him and turned to listen to Sanderson—as the evening resumed itself, as couples shuffled on the floor, as the band like a machine drummed out its honey-thick noise, as the dark-haired frightened-eyed waiters slammed in and out of the kitchen door.

"It's funny," Sanderson was saying, "how they go at it. No holds barred, that's a fact. But d'you know, all the time those two bitches were at it I was thinking of my old missus? She's a Theosophist. No lie, a Theosophist. And you know what I was thinking? I was thinking when a woman gets an idea in her head, it's all or nothing. There's the parallel. Now my old girl hardly thinks of anything else but this stunt of hers. Out at her meetings, getting her groups together, talking it out with this or that fellow-theo-ossified as I call it—take my advice, young man, don't go for a thinking woman, there's plenty run down the dumb ones but I don't know so much, get one that thinks, and where are you? In the old Acacia Room, like me! Nothing else to do, old boy. Of course"—he paused as some idea struck him—"there's Arthur, too. Arthur might have something to do with it—"

"Arthur? Arthur who?"

Sanderson giggled: "Our Thermometer, eh? No, not that, old boy. Arthur's my old tortoise."

Matthew was getting muddled. He had winced at Sanderson calling the hostesses "bitches": he had been lifted by being called "young man"—important now. Now he was down again with this Arthur.

"It's this old tortoise I have. Like a very old man Arthur is—dragging about all day doing nothing with a great shell on his back . . . ever thought what your own shell would feel like old boy? It'd be like having your great toe-nail swell up and grow all over you. That's what I think. Something you can't feel like your old toe-nail, but you know it's yours, see? Never mind, that's not what I'm getting at. It's something else about Arthur that gets *me* down."

Sanderson stopped to light a cigar. Matthew waited. He saw Lily had picked every bit off the haddock bone. Was she kept hungry then? Or was it nerves?

"It's this," said Sanderson. "Arthur yawns. Here's old Arthur, eh? Arthur with damn-all to do for a hundred years, Arthur with his toe-nail on his back—Arthur suddenly interrupts himself. He stops. He looks around slowly—bored to death—and then ever so quietly, shuts his eyes, and opens his little pink mouth, and yawns, *yawns* dammit, a long, slow Godforsaken yawn . . . I tell you, it turns me up. It showed me, once and for all, how boring it is to be bored. So I stopped stopping alone at home and here I am."

Sanderson laughed amiably, a man who has confided a weakness with which he is rather pleased. Matthew did not know what to say. "I've never had a tortoise," he said.

Sanderson looked startled. It had sounded like no ordinary gambit of tortoise-talk but instead a most plaintive appeal; much of Matthew's loneliness and dissatisfaction with the evening had gone into the simple remark.

"I shouldn't worry, old man," Sanderson said, plainly touched but trying to be jovial, filling the glasses. "I shouldn't worry too much about *that*."

Then Matthew pulled himself together and feeling low as a little detective asked Sanderson: "That girl you were with—isn't Lily her name?—looked quite a— a smasher."

"Lily?" Sanderson said. "Oh, Liliane. Yes, she's a good-looker all right. Nice girl, too. Very nice girl, that."

Nice? Nice in what way? Nice to—whom? Or nice?

Sanderson sighed: "But I expect she's no better than she should be."

"What?"

"I said, she's probably no better than—"

Matthew smiled immense relief: "Then—you don't actually *know*?"

"Don't know what?"

It was too intimate. He could not put it into plain words. He caught at a drowning straw: "What that means. That phrase you used. She's no better than she should be? What should she be? What's she no better than?"

Sanderson repeated the phrase to himself, raised his

eyebrows, took the cigar from his mouth which remained open in a little surprised "o" shape. "D'you know, I don't know?" he said.

Then he sat there pondering, looking a little frightened, repeating the words over to himself.

Matthew expanded with relief. So it was all right! Lily was all right! And with Sanderson too—a "regular"!

Relieved he suddenly felt tired. No point in staying. The evening was somehow rounded off. He thanked Sanderson, asked for his bill and began to leave. "Don't worry about Arthur too much," he said, looking at Sanderson with something like love, "they're rather fond of a bit of shut-eye. Like yours truly," he ended with a fine attempt at joviality, and left.

It was a wild, raining night. The street-lamps blinked in the flying air. A late bus came scudding by, itself like a great gust of wind. The air smelled of winter again, a cold smell of beer and coal-smoke invigorated the wet brown pavements. He buttoned up his coat tight, looked up and down for a taxi, and decided to walk. Plodding along the pavement, his spirits dropped again; relief had knocked the spur of hope out of him.

TEN

NEXT MORNING he sat wondering and fidgeting again. A normal course might have been to pick up the telephone and ask Lily how her sister was, trusting she was recovered, hoping Lily was not too tired. Not Matthew. His fingers itched for it, but every time the little black talking-box bared its teeth.

For might not Lily be embarrassed by her sister's behaviour? Might it not be wiser to wait, forget the affair, let sleeping dogs lie? They might indeed still be sleeping it off: (One of her curtains was drawn aside—but perhaps for the night air?) And was he, in any case, quite forgiven for his appearance at the Acacia Room? He had certainly not forgiven himself for his guilty detective work with Sanderson. And then Dawn—he'd be in particularly bad odour with Dawn? Refusing to be provoked by her had certainly led to the fight— Dawn's temper had had to erupt somewhere, he could see that clearly now—but would not Dawn also connect him with it? Through her morning mists? And perhaps—and this was the truly appalling thought—would she not retail to Lily how he had said he had wanted to marry her? And had he? It was awfully muddled. He felt almost as if he had said it. And then—did he want to say it? And what about Lily—what had she said? I do too, she had said. I do too. It reverberated in his mind.

Reverberated as the image of those two wrestling, the pink and the black, and somehow mixed up in the wrestling the words Lily and Dawn, Lily and Dawn . . . mixed more in mind precisely now that they must be separated, the names cast apart, the flesh differentiated—that Dawn and Lily shared the same blood was, with marriage in the air, intolerable. He sat concentrating on all differences between them, skin and colour and shape, wishing them different.

But all of us, he got to thinking, are a lot more different from each other than we think we are. Put a six-foot-six drum major alive with ginger moustaches against a small bald post office clerk: would a benign observer from Mars think them to be of the same race? Yet we are the ones to giggle at a couple of dogs, a mastiff and a maltese, when they recognize each other instantly as "dogs." We are the wonders who wonder at two insects on a leaf—and Matthew looked down at the gardens where so often he had observed the small and intricate leaf-life—one a black giant horned and armoured, the other a thin-winged delicacy with a foal's long-limbed stagger, we wonder that two such divergent creatures should amble past each other, each on its equable errand, each seeing nothing peculiar in the appearance of the other. Perhaps such insects and such dogs would be equally amused to see the great

black-haired Estelle and Dawn's pink brawn interlaced
in the fight, under the impression, poor dears, that
they were of the same genus. Such thoughtful creatures would die, surely, laughing, at the conception of
Lily and Dawn as *sisters?*

People, he thought, looking over at all the regular
windows with their irregular curtains—lace here, satin
there, here pink cotton like an old dressing-gown, and
there not even curtains at all but white slatted blinds—
all so different, yet set about a convention of oval
mirror-backs where arms waved beneath lamps swimming gold as fishbowls hung in the air. Such sameness,
such difference. Peas as different as chalk from cheese.
And above them their roof-furniture—queer-shaped
funnels and cowls and aerials like a motionless projec-
tion of individuality, strange creatures strutting high
against the sky and silently hooting their freedom above
the pachyderm houses.

No, people are never the same. Nor do things stop
still with people; it's change, change, change all the
way round. From week to week they change, or circumstances change them, and everyone else has to
change along with them. Here's Lily, another person to
him this week. And dear old Leslie—now no more than
a thorn in his side because of an upstairs window. And
old Uncle Hugh—quite different, gabbling all by himself into a steel box. All changed. And this, he thought
with an angry glance at the peaceable brickscape, at a
time when he had sat himself down for a couple of
months of rest and reorientation, at a time of life pointing towards forty when he had wanted to settle some

of the questions inside himself, yes, for the few sabbatical weeks at a climacteric point, given this chance that is every man's desire—and look what had happened! People had got at him.

Marriage, he thought.

Why had he not thought of marriage before?

Why, come to that, had he not thought of contriving an affair with Lily?

What is called an overt sexual approach had not occurred to him. Why not? Surely sex was natural between the sexes? Surely, at least, he ought to have thought of it?

But he had to face it, he had not thought of it. He had felt simply and blessedly again like a boy swept into an entrancing, sacred hero-worship. But this was a heroine! What had she felt? The thought came suddenly, and it appalled: Had she expected more? Was she insulted? Once more it crossed his mind that she looked "boyish." Was this then the message of his climacteric, was he a very changed man?

It did not feel so. And this brought him to the main problem—age. He had not thought of her as a woman, but as a girl, because he was so much older himself. But then, was he? He remembered how very old he had felt at twenty. But step up the years, and there would Lily be at thirty and he getting on for fifty. A big difference.

And marriage?

"Why aren't you married?" he shot at Leslie swaying in with an unwanted tray of milk.

Leslie looked as if he had been hit between the eyes.

"Me?" he said.

"Never thought of it, eh?"

He put the tray down. "I like Leslie," he said and from custom went over to the window. Matthew saw haloed by window-light the frayed jacket. He changed his tone, and brought the question to where he wanted it: "What would you say if I was to get married?"

Leslie turned and stared, his face dark as a painting against the light.

"Two can live cheaper than one," he said, "I don't think."

"No, seriously."

"Who's the lucky lady? Mrs. Orme?"

"That is, I mean, if she'll have me . . . " and Matthew's stomach gave a little jump.

"By the way," Leslie said, "I suppose you *have* seen our Orme this morning? You've heard the great news?"

Matthew hardly heard: "You know whom I'm talking of. Would you call it mad of me? At my age?" The phrase sounded itself mad—"at my age!" But there was no other.

Leslie pulled at a moustache: "Well," he said, "I only thought you'd be interested. It's going to turn us upside down here right enough . . . just you wait a few hours!" But then what Matthew had been saying jerked the other half of his mind alive: "You mean—old Lily?"

Matthew nodded and watched him carefully. But it was a dealer's face, and at the offer of a new idea automatically deepened its gloom.

"She's a very nice girl," he said, "I should go ahead."

"But at my age?" Matthew protested.

"She's taken ten years off it already."

Matthew looked, off hand, down at the carpet: "It doesn't look to you like—baby-snatching?"

Leslie sighed. "What baby? No offence, mind."

"When I'm sixty she'll only be forty."

"You'll both be as young as you feel. Nobody ever stops saying that. Go ahead and good luck. This puts me out of a job."

"Oh, we'll see to that somehow. . . . "

"You've popped the question then?"

"Not exactly."

"Then go in and get done with it, boy."

Matthew glanced uneasily out of the window. She was not there. He was horrified less at Leslie's direct-ness than at the finality of it. He wanted the thing dis-cussed, reviewed, talked over: not simplified. He hedged.

"But I hardly know her."

Leslie frowned: "And what in old Harry's name was you doing covered in them pigeons, I'd like to know?" The photograph of them taken in Trafalgar Square, birds all over, smiled like a honeymoon from the desk. "What have you been up to these last weeks?" Leslie accused darkly.

Matthew drew a long breath and said, broadly, gen-erously: "I suppose I've been doing what the next fel-low does. I've been hanging about getting to know someone I knew all the time." He added quickly: "You only get action in films and so on. Life's different. You hang about a lot."

"What about Dawn?" Leslie said. "Nice comfortable kind of sister-in-law, eh?"

"You don't take that sort of thing into consideration."

"You'll be taking her into the spare bedroom, though."

"Really—it doesn't matter. Though I agree she's hell. You don't know what happened last night."

He told Leslie about the fight, and across the down-drawn face a gleam of enthusiasm spread and wanly flourished. "That's trouble all right," he said. "She'll be teaching your Lil all the wrinkles. I wouldn't be you coming in late with a few beers under your belt."

"Seriously," Matthew said, "you've just about hit what's worrying me. If Lily goes on living with that awful woman, she'll get more and more influenced. It's like that with an elder sister. The kid's so young."

He sat up and a dreadful instinct began to quicken in him: "She can't go on living there!" he said. "If only for that reason, I ought to. . . . "

Leslie snapped in quickly: "Give her a job. You could do that easily."

"Job?"

"What d'you call it—market research. Anything like that. Knocking on doors and bothering people."

"Lily?"

There was a knock and Mrs. Orme's face appeared round the door. "Excuse me, but they've found some more pieces, they say," she said.

"No!" Leslie shouted.

"Yes," Mrs. Orme whispered, a look of awe drawing her primly painted face.

Leslie turned on Matthew. "Look, you *must* listen to Mrs. Orme, Matthew," he said. "It's the ruddy end! They've found . . . "

But Matthew stopped him short. "I don't want to know anything. I've got to *think*, can't you see?"

"But Matthew," Leslie said, "this is *urgent,* man!"

Matthew only waved him away. Leslie gave a hopeless shrug and went to the door. "You'll know soon enough," he muttered as he left.

What Matthew wanted to think about now was this; "I ought to marry Lily to get her away from Dawn." Quite seriously he set himself to think of it this way. It was a reason-for, and his mind, searching for conflict, suspicious of simplicity, clutched at it.

He sat trying to weigh and juggle as if this were not love so much as a series of tactical positions. He should marry her because of the difference in their ages. He should marry her because she needed him—she must be protected against Dawn. But on the other hand, as Leslie had suggested, he might simply get her a job? But would that be thorough enough? And as far as age came into it—was he not less worried on the physical score as on some final incompatibility of understanding and tastes? However—one married a Bulgar and was fairly happy?

He sat there crossing and uncrossing his mind. Here was conflict at last, a tangible obstacle to be tried and overcome. And the very complication appealed—his tactical mind preferred to make a decision not for one but for a whole subterfuge of different reasons. His eyes wandered away about the room, strayed over the dark lace curtains, strayed on the high gold-glinting bookshelves. There, behind these bindings, he thought, were thousands of words on marriage—discourses, apothegms, wisdom of all kinds. "Marriages are the long expirations of a moment's imprudence. You cannot be frivolous about your own freedom." "The dread of loneliness is greater than the fear of bondage, so we get married." "I got married because I was afraid of freedom." And so on. All of them wise, none of them any real good. No, he had sadly to return to a simplicity. You get married because you want to be together: without conditions; for the rest of life. One of the plainest of plain facts was that he wanted to be, all of the time, with Lily.

He felt that at this point he should leap from his chair with a wild joy—this beautiful discovery made! But he did not. It rather depressed him. And it was exactly the simplicity that he found depressing; or that perhaps, simply, unseated him. He wanted a hurdle. He wanted to be stopped. He wanted what happened in other love affairs. He wanted to hunt, he wanted to fight.

He found himself staring into the side-eye of a thickset black bird advertising fountain pens. Somehow the brochure had got off the desk and into his hands. The bird was looking at a row of fountain pens with an expression of wholly malevolent joy, its eye white and wide, its beak open to let red script caw forth. "The Early Bird gets the Pen."

Why, his mind vaguely questioned, should such a bird want a pen? He saw brittle bits of black plastic caught in the bird's beak, the gold nib winking as it slid down by its darkly tettering little uvula—and suddenly he remembered the blackbird that had settled, weeks ago, on his window-sill as he had leapt back into the room at his first sight of her over at her window.

It seemed suddenly significant! Significant too this message "The Early Bird." He looked up startled, then across to her window. And there she was again! For the first time that morning leaning far out, out in the clear grey light, looking along the gardens in the Tiger-pants direction.

She looked a long grey way away. And he suddenly woke up to the fact that all these thoughts of marriage were absurdly presumptive, they were simply friends newly met, they had had a good time and liked each other. And that "I-do-too" of hers—anyone might say it, it was just kindness. He cursed his lack of humility. It had looked so easy—of course it had looked easy. And when anything looks easy—smell for danger: particularly for the danger of your fatheaded old mind off its guard.

He had counted on one Lily—but there might be fifty different Lilies, he thought. And just then, as the daylight washed through him, he became conscious of a bewildering illusion—for there were in fact fifty Lilies all over those façades opposite . . . no, not Lilies, but figures like Lily's, people all over leaning out of other windows, all peering in the same direction. Something was afoot along the gardens.

Seeing her, his hand had reached again for the tele-

phone. But then it occurred to him to pull up the sash
and for once risk Lily looking over to him—he could
point at the telephone and make sure she would
answer it.

But Lily was too occupied with what all were looking at, a group of men in mackintoshes digging at the
end of the Average Housewife's—a Mrs. Mortimer's—
garden. Behind them, on the concrete among battered
toys, there stood, motionless and like a big toy himself,
a dark blue policeman.

Something sharp hit Matthew on the head, bounced
off, and fell to the garden. It was a dry crust of bread.
Sparrows, he knew from long afternoons in a deckchair, dropped these hurtful little crusts. If he looked
up, he would see a sparrow looking at him sideways
from the gutter above, cheek inclined against the sky.
So he did not look up. And another crust fell.

Above, where he had expected beady eyes and beak,
there peered, upside down, Leslie's much larger face:
accompanied by Mrs. Orme's half profile, immense
from beneath as a goddess's.

Leslie bent his hand round his mouth to baffle a
huge whisper that echoed over the gardens like a
hunter's cry: "They've found a foot!"

Matthew glanced nervously over at the McGhee's
window. But nobody seemed to have heard, all were
too fascinated by the little group of men digging.

"Who have?" he said up to Leslie.

"The police, who else?"

Mrs. Orme's voice came down tragic, intoning as at

a seance: "Her pieces," she said, "that they're digging for!"

"Good God!"

The suggestion of murder, of newsprint murder happened near, very near, shaded the air palpably, like a cooking smell, like a shadow-creeping cloud.

"Who is it?" he whispered up to Leslie.

"Nobody knows. But it's Mrs. Average H.W.'s garden."

"Not their children!" Matthew cried.

Mrs. Orme intoned down: "It's a grown woman's foot. They say she's away on holiday."

"He was growing marrows there," Leslie added, "prize vegetable marrows."

"A fine holiday *she's* having," Mrs. Orme darkly said.

"You don't think . . . ?" Matthew saw again like a brightlit advertisement photograph the well-known figure of Mrs. Mortimer hanging out clothes, face so bright, apron smiling in the fresh morning light, lips pining for the Argentine. "But there never *was* such a happy family!"

"No one's said anything yet," Leslie said. "It started this morning. The papers may have it by lunchtime. It's only that Baldy with his rose-squirt got the dope—he's still down there now, you can see him."

And it was true, the little man whose face no one had ever properly seen, but whose bald dome and pest syringe were so well known—he was crouched down among forsythia with his ear pressed just under the level of the cat-walk wall. A storey above, Miss Tigerpants's falsies draped in shocking-pink rose and fell breathfully, Poo her poodle quivering on the ledge beside. Next window one back—Lily (Where was Dawn? Asleep? Unheeding?) . . . and then scattered at windows all along the façade others, all looking the one way, so that they looked like a chorus set at windows in a theatre backcloth all schooled to do the same thing.

The day was dingy, rain in the night had blackened trees and walls. No sun—but high grey flying clouds, spirited rags against the bath-water sky beyond. It must have been muddy digging.

Yet the air was warm, and the fresh atmosphere of spring with leaves greening everywhere nevertheless enlivened the morning. There was an echo in the air and one could just hear the muffled ring of the policemen's spades, the mackintoshed murmur of the big detectives. But up from the next garden beneath, that which dripped with laurel, voices of other mackintoshed men rose plain. They had with them this morning a man in a tweed overcoat. "It's a *nice* little patch of garden," they were saying, "and you've got your dining-room looking out. Coat of fresh paint too." And to a tweeded murmur: "Bless us—a little damp on the walls? But you can't expect different. All these houses the same, you know."

A new life beginning here, Matthew thought, someone moving in? Here where the laurel dripped and murder should have been done—why, even these house agents masqueraded as raincoated detectives bunched whispering! . . . and over there a life ended among the brightly concreted crazy paving and the lusty beans, the marrows, the daily washing hung to a radio song!

"How did they get on to it?" Matthew called up. "Where's the husband? Who started them off?"

"The pussies," Leslie said. "The pussies going about their business so neat and clean. They got the scent all right. I'll bet it was Dupont, the hungry thing."

"Oh be quiet, Mr. Lovelace!" Mrs. Orme said, her eyes shining.

Matthew still hung on the sill. It was difficult to see anything much, impossible to stop looking. The little group digging cast a shadow over all. Yet simply to look at them, they might have been men at a gas main.

Now it seemed cruel to telephone and thus interrupt Lily—but of course he wanted desperately to do so: also . . . was it right for Lily to be so taken up with such an unsavoury business, was this her sweet character?

Yet she was one of many. And down below, through criss-cross fencing and wire and creeper, people were talking to each other, friends at last! It might suddenly have been an outer suburb, and these people suddenly like the suburban folk they scorn, human enough at last to borrow mowers or pass the time of day.

He picked up the telephone. He saw Lily hear the bell, lean forward anxiously for a last look, then disappear. He hated interrupting her. He felt acutely this least discomfiture of her—the more so when he heard the irritation in her voice. So he pretended he wanted the Metropolitan Water Board.

She answered that yes she was the Water Board and

she'd send over and drown him it he tried to fool her like that, she knew his voice quite well.

She knew his voice! That was wonderful! He did not reflect that the same might be true of her grocer's—but instead, delighted, elated, he asked her how she was? And Dawn?

"No bones broken," was the contained reply.

Either Lily was untouched by the event, or determined that he should not intrude upon a matter, possibly, of family pride.

"But," she went on, "bones is rather near the knuckle this morning. I suppose you've heard?"

So she had never looked across to see if he were looking?

"I hope you're not too upset," he said, knowing she was not, hoping she might be.

"It's having to look that's so dreadful, apart from—"

"Can we have lunch?" he said.

"Lunch?" she said. "Eat?"

Was she then after all upset? No. A touch of a laugh somewhere as: "Not to-day. There's a certain individual here needs looking after."

"Oh."

"She's only a little shaky. Needs a sister's hand. I'm sorry, I'd have loved to . . . incidentally you're not popular there," she added.

"But I *must* see you."

"I know, Matthew."

"Then dinner? Couldn't we . . . ?"

"I'll try. I *will* try."

Her voice was soft; and understanding: and almost

urgent. He then said what was a simple but perhaps the most direct and open thing, for him, that he had ever said to her: "Come to the window, just once—and wave?"

There was only a pause—and then she said awkwardly: "I'm sorry—she's calling. I can't." And, with a goodbye, rang off.

He was left excluded. She would probably telephone soon—but that one concession had been refused. Over the gulf of gardens he felt painfully the city's closed life, the bitterness of the human honeycomb.

He went over to the window again and looked down at the digging. The little group bent their khaki backs and muddily sifted. The one uniformed policeman still stood like an entranced blue-domed doll. And up above, from a little frilled iron funnel in the wall, steam came wisping white: on the second floor of the same house the pale shape of a naked body flowered against frosted glass, blushed pink, disappeared. Someone having a bath. A dismembered body in the vegetable bed; and a moving body, uncut, naked and alive, weaving about the bathroom above! It was too immodest, it called for towels, shrouds. He turned away, and approached his own face in the deep, clear mahogany-framed mirror. Not lines of age but grooves of endurance accused him; what had been ten years ago a rounded face had now lengthened—you looked at it up and down now. His eyes stared back with a cold penetration that looked too much like the wisdom of age.

Of course, he thought, the eyebrows and odd bits of hair tend to grow longer and thicker with the years,

and that does something to the eyes. But—were those
pouches forming beneath? Or simply grey circles? He
looked hard, and beside what was a quite amiable face,
a little hardened by his late-thirties, in which he chose
now to scent some terrible ravage of time—beside this
he placed Lily's face, its cream of skin, its dispassionate
youth, its brown eyes under blonde hair so like a soft
animal's. How could this hard thing of his presume
upon such purity?

He felt he was falling to pieces already. There was
the coming and going, like a grisly little tinkerbell, of
the ulcer inside him. And the eczema. And sometimes
an audible snap as a bone moved into unusual action.
And his wind—could he run upstairs without discomfort? He suddenly asked himself: Would she want to go
dancing much?

The idea of dancing inspired a particular terror. It
symbolized all the eagerness and hope of youth. A
kind of agony overcame him; there in his suit—a quietly
dressed citizen of the daily world whose face could
never show much emotion—he suffered a sudden wild-
ness of spirit, an anguish. Usually resigned he felt suddenly restrained. He looked down at his daylight suit.
What was needed was action—a scarlet cloak! Yet all
he could do was wait for a telephone bell to ring! He
stared with hate at the squat black instrument, at least
it should have been white and set on a sable rug and
smelling of opoponax or something, anything, anything. . . .

It did not ring for a full half-hour. He went to the
window again. A new figure stood in the garden where

they were digging, a more important-looking detective
who wore above his mackintosh a black homburg hat.
This man had a malacca stick, whose handle he held
curved round the brim of his hat to hold it down in the
wind—he stood there holding a malacca question-mark
to his head. Someone had turned up a wireless, and between snatches of music an announcer's voice enun-
ciated clearly, giving the names of housewives who had
asked for their favourite records: *I'm in the Mink,
Home Sweet Home, The Nutcracker Suite.* "Mrs.
Martin of twenty-three Maidstone Villas, Reddicap,
Glamorganshire. Mrs. A. Tomlin, twenty-seven Cundy
Street, South Shields. Mrs. Polly Burton and her friend
'Molly'—Polly and Molly, eh?—both of Strathspey
Villas, Trowbridge, Hants." It was a repeat of Housewives' Choice. Parlours and kitchen, kirbies and cosies
intoned their sunny requiem over this poor dead one,
houselife done.

He turned sourly away—a fine setting for his ro-
mance! . . . and pulled the sash down on it all . . . when
his fingers on the window brought to mind something
else, a lighter thought—for he suddenly saw how, when
the sun would set above the housetop opposite, then
the last gilded rays would flash into fire the western
window he held in his hands, his window, and thus
like a searchlight would beam across to hers, there to
make some delicate pattern of dying light on her wall,
pink and gold light, shadows of leaves and lace, a tired
and lovely light at the ending of day. His window
gave that to her.

Then Leslie burst in waving the lunchtime paper.

"It's Ma Mortimer all right," he said. "Dad's disappeared. Would you ever have thought it? *That* happy pair!"

Matthew said, "Look, Leslie, I'm a bit busy just now—"

"She with her washing and him pottering about the garden . . . if ever you saw the perfect—"

"Are they sure it's her?"

"They don't say they want to interview Madame, oh no they want *him*."

Matthew suddenly shivered: "It makes you hate him, really *hate* . . . it turns your lip."

"All the same, I'd like to have seen the look of surprise on her face when he came at her. With a chopper."

"Look, Les—I said I was busy. . . . "

The cheerful look left Leslie's eye: "Well we're in for a fine time, reporters and rubbernecks, a good thing it's not next-door, you'd have them getting in over the fence. It'll give the place a bad name. We're done for socially, old boy."

Matthew looked down in the garden, where people were at last talking to each other. "I don't know," he said, watching Mrs. Peabasin talking at ease to Baldy, and the couple on the left smiling for the first time; "I'd say it's made us socially."

"It's an ill wind . . . " Leslie sighed.

And then the telephone bell rang, and her voice came fresh against the grey dustbin day of digging. He suddenly found himself asking her exactly what first came to mind: "Do you like dancing?"

"Well, I'm rather in the trade you know."

He had quite forgotten that. That was awful.

"But do you *really* like it?"

"Why? You off dancing again tonight? Think of my poor feet, please."

"Oh bless you, you're free then. . . . "

And then they arranged to dine. He was left high on that, but low on this point of dancing. Poor feet or not, people often did what they say they dislike because deep down they do like it. Familiarity breeds only a veneer of contempt—the complaining cashier really likes the feel of banknotes: and how many dustmen are firm analerotic?

But he stopped his mind wandering and tried to concentrate. Age. *Age.* That was the vital point. He was aware he had liked to think of himself as older than he was. But how about a double-deception—perhaps that was simply an involved way of imagining himself younger than he really was. How about that? He remembered how in the last years middle-aged people had come to look of indeterminate age. Previously he could have separated forty from fifty at a glance. Not now. Looking at his own face in the mirror, had he grown accustomed to the crack and crust of the years? Did he dig out for his own eyes only some general feature of youth behind the rot?

That evening they dined early in a small restaurant on the other side of the town, and to meet her Ligne walked through a large square of Georgian building now let as offices.

Each tall regular window shone bright with yellow light, as if the whole square had been given over that night to a ball. At last a place without curtains! The windows were alive! There was a bustle of people—possibly carrying files or bending at desks—but who looked at a distance simply like people caught up in a golden occasion.

Above the rooftops the pale turquoise and coral sky was streaked with the fabulous trails of past aeroplanes. He felt the evening glitter of motor traffic and the sense of hurry and direction of those passing-by—and remembered how in the past, when he walked alone among such evening excitation, the sense of exclusion was stronger than drawn curtains. All lights on, all windows open—yet he alone left out! . . . But now going to meet her he could join in complicity with the lights, he was part of the ball and, passing through the square, a man in an ordinary suit, he bubbled inside with joy and premonition.

They dined off twice-cooked food at a high price, and wandered out afterwards into an evening still warm from the spring day.

Much, but to little point, had been said. What moved between them more than words were expressions of face. Besides, Matthew had not wanted to mix anything too serious with moussaka and zabaglione. This must be kept for a moment without waiters. Murder and Dawn's fight had taken them through the meal.

But now what was repressed leaped to get out; they

wandered, terribly arm in arm, savouring slowly one street and then another, intimate their presence, until a space appeared still overgrown with tall brown weeds from the previous autumn, an overgrowth among torn railings—and inside it a path among black and white tombstones. They wandered in, trespassing on the night, and found a seat quite hidden from the street.

Dark walls formed a corner, no light fell from windows, the jungle of weeds and saplings rose against only a faded far away glow; the gravestones, some soot-black and others cleaned by wind and wash, sat humped like monstrous black and white cats and improved the silence. There was a sense of solitude and separation from the streets. Both Lily and Matthew pretended to shiver in the warm air as a gesture against sitting for long, and then sat.

But at last alone Matthew did not know what to say. The old ease between them seemed to have gone. There was this new and immense idea of marriage. Was he there to propose to her? If not—then why not? What he did feel strongly was a common enough feeling—that a move in some direction must be made, that things can never be left, good as they are, to stand still.

Lily must have been equally nervous. She had begun to talk too brightly—something about the black and white tombstones: "If you were in a white tie, and I in a black evening dress and we had a few dalmatians. . . . " But was she only enjoying, as youth does, the idea of trespass? While he was in a mild way disturbed by it? . . . age and youth again . . . but swelling in his mind was the great and immediate urgent need to say what he had to say himself and which now he gave up putting into words at all—other than one, which, taking suddenly her hand in his and gathering her closer to him, he spoke at her, stroking it on his tongue like a deep conspiracy, like a libation, her name, a leaven of love: "Lily."

She stopped speaking, nestled herself closer, made her hand a presence warm in his. To say a name is to say all. The word that she must a million times have heard before broke down all tensions between them; much more than a word was articulate.

There rattled in his throat the beginnings of all he wanted to say, the old impossible phrases, "How wonderful it was to hear what you said last night"—"did you really mean it?"—"you do like me a little?"—lover's language when self-consciousness at last lifts itself away, as it should do and as it usually does—but not with Matthew who was struck dumb by their platitude and who now ground them all down into one infallible one, the greatest of all, even then grafting on blasphemy to greaten it: "God, how I love you!" And as he said it, and felt truly the humility that redeems so egoist a statement, the swearing of "God" turned to invocation.

Yet still the moment before their lips touched he paused—for now, was it not now the moment to speak what he really had to say, to propose? Somehow—before they kissed?

Now?

Not.

Her hair breathed up smelling close, her girl's soft

waiting silence came to him, they were two together
hidden in a weedgrown graveyard, in warm night alone
to conduct themselves as they should and wanted—
and still he had to get caught up in the changing
comedy of manners, to hear the echo of a now distant
past where the proposal went before the kiss and the
man besought on bended knee—yet hearing this from
a living present, where manners preferred exactly the
opposite, when one must kiss first before such words
can be thought to be spoken. Strung up thus between
two suitabilities, both right, he at last dropped to earth
as he should, to the present earth, and their four lips
closed together excluding like a close photograph their
wider faces and the night.

During that second of no-touch, then touch, it was
all changed: the whole breath of living was balanced
high like a rock on a pinnacle, possibly to move this
way, possibly that, at the tremor of whatever breath
should blow across—and then his life and blood poised
between her as person and her as woman came
rumbling down as the scent and warmth and softness
came up and she seemed to fold into him, becoming
instantly age, not youth, ageless age.

They kissed, and their arms embraced their bodies,
and it grew warmer, and their faces parted and they
smiled close and said their names before lips still open
on names met again, and the night went out, and hands
at ends of arms stroked and moved like hands on their
own, bent only on their natural purpose, so that with
no calculating thought his hand found her breast and
for a little was content to stay there, content on its

round completeness, and all the time their closeness
compounded, they grew warmer, lost sense as their
senses rose and there swelled first in Matthew the hot
tenderness to protect and taste this his beloved, yet
hard above it that other wild savage will to break and
tear apart fiercely, to hurt and to eat, body-hot, hand-
mad, headlong, headlost.

Clothes and buttons, buttons and clothes fingered
fumbling to fall apart, so quick the two to press together—yet in all that dark and rising blood, away as
two are far beyond all, a single cat's thin mew pierced
between them, so small a sound but through what
pounded like hot thunder in their ears this little sound
did come, and astonished, as if they had been asleep,
now waking slowly, they looked down and saw beneath
them the small face of grey fur, eyes asking, back
bunching, tail up straight as a voice, and again from so
small but assured a personality came the mew, a delicate and urgent appeal. . . .

Grey as a shadow it primped itself high on its legs
and rubbed against Lily's; its eyes caught light from
somewhere and glinted like goggles; with an easy
spring it jumped onto their one lap.

Waking to what they were doing washed down like
cold rain. Wanting to shooo it away, he could not.
Waking more clearly each moment to what had happened, he could not so obviously clear the field for
more. Instead he put out his hand, that had just stroked
Lily, to stroke the cat.

The cat purred but did not settle itself, it began
walking round and round on their one lap, flexing its

big paws—and then began a forceful treading motion.

"Shoooooo!" Lily cried instantly, pushing it straight off. "Claws!"

Thanking God for a woman and her clothes he laughed, and she murmured, "Poor thing, he's hungry," as he took her in his arms again and once more they kissed.

But now it was different.

Heads lost were cleared, it was as soft and beautiful, as loving, but he felt now she had a constraint about her. Or he had? When he put his hand on her breast again, now knowing it, she put hers over his and he did not know whether this was to hold his hand there or perhaps in a moment push it away.

It came to him then that if the proposal comes after the kiss, now was the time to make it. He wanted to tell her how much he loved and loved her—but a proposal seemed so much a proposition—could such a moment be really right?—was it not still too tensed?—and in any case, that cat was back, or it had never gone away, it was rubbing and pressing and purring loud like a little engine, and how could he say such things with this cat there?

And suddenly his stomach bit at him again. Tension, moussaka—an absurd dish for him to choose. The blood drained from his face, and the dreadfully dull pain began dragging at his strength. She suddenly drew closer to him shivering: "I'm cold, darling."

So they must go?

It was all over? The evening, the graveyard, the warmth? No more time, no *time*—and feeling it all tick away he opened his mouth to cheat the moment, seize it, hold it—and found himself not saying the words so difficult to find but offering her a job.

Would she like to go from door to door asking housewives whether they found cheese indigestible? Would she like to find out how many grates were polished in a square quarter mile of Birmingham? It sounded boring, but . . .

She started shaking quietly in the half-dark. Crying? "You *are* extraordinary," she said at last, "I thought you were going to say something quite different." Laughing?

He stiffened, caught out. Had she then suspected, even expected, what he had first had in mind? Was she waiting, quietly helping? Was there never going to be a single obstacle, could she not set up a single, natural hurdle?

"What? What was I going to say?" he said.

"Never you mind."

He began again, he had to go on now: "It's a good kind of job. It doesn't tie you to an office. The pay's not wonderful, but I'd see you got the most possible."

"It's all so sudden," she whispered.

"Well, there it is. Any day you like."

"May I," she said softly in that darkness, pressed close to him, "may I—have time to think it over?"

"Of course. Of course."

She was shaking again. He was not sure what was going on. The cat sprang up suddenly onto their lap. Perhaps it was this?

"It's very sweet of you," she said. "And I'm terribly—honoured."

"Oh *quiet*," he said and kissed her again and then they shook the cat off and got up.

He was desperate to get away from the seat, something should have been said and something had been said, it had put an end to the seat, no more could be said or done there—but nevertheless as they walked out into the lamplit street she clung closely on his arm, and it was altogether different, for much, however muddled, had passed between them.

Much later that night he put out more food on the cats' plate in the garden than ever before. It was a visiting cats' plate—for Dupont and the Ginger and others—but that night he put down the food as a thank-offering. He was now appalled at what might have happened had that cat not interrupted them. His stomach flinched cold with awe, as one might think afterwards of a road accident just averted, terror and thanks secreted at the same moment. It did not bear thinking of, he thought of it and thought of it and marvelled at his terror, grateful to find himself neither puritan nor chivalrist but simply at last a man who wanted to keep one compartment sacrosanct, against all instinct and with every intuition.

◆

ELEVEN

◆

AND AS I SAID, said Leslie, those pieces of housewife they dug up changed everything. The neighbourhood went plumb crazy. Half a million sentimental citizens came rubber-nosing in. Home wasn't home any more. No holding Mrs. Orme. Even old Mattie was like a cat on hot bricks. But I'll come to him later.

The old Goat went mad. Everybody had their own story—it was like the bombs again. Not a soul but hadn't got this or that straight from the horse's mouth, the milkman's I presume, or knew somebody who knew somebody who knew the backside of a copper's aunt. People you never saw came in for a pint—old Tiger-pants and for the love of God Mrs. Peabasin. All that about a pub being the common man's parliament came true as your eye. And you know what rumour was? It was rife. The ladies had something to chat about for once all right—you never saw the shops so full—though I will say they looked a bit white round the gills walking about with their baskets very stern. Someone said there was a brisk sale in the chopper line down the oil-shop. What I do know is Old Straw the fishmonger,

[200]

who came in evenings for a pint, told us how he'd not sold a cod's head in days—no one liked to ask for Pussy's Pieces now.

But for all that, none of us in our hearts thought it quite so funny. Better in the News than on your door-step, there was a kind of shadow about, you had a dirty feeling.

And what worried everyone uppermost was how the deceased—that was what they called her now, nobody liked to say her name—how she'd never been heard to have a quarrel with her old man. There were many about knew the Mortimers. Never an ill word spoken. An ideal couple, they said. The deceased was always bright as a new pin, always smiling, a cheery word for everyone. Her hubby was a steady fellow keen on his garden, a help in the home they said, took his turn with the kids and the cleaning and all. Had a job down the coal-yard, in the office there, used to sit all day with his kitchen nuts blazing in the grate making out your bills. Nice safe job, went up a bit every year or two, nothing wrong there.

Then we began to hear what it was all about. And you'll never believe it.

First, they picked him up. Inside twenty-four hours. No trouble, came quiet as a lamb. Said he'd been wait-ing for them, hadn't known quite what to do, couldn't work it out for himself, felt muddled. Found him sitting under Eros, if you please.

Of course everybody was a bit disappointed. I think they'd've liked a bit of a chase, they'd have liked him to disappear for a bit—say, get picked up in Scarborough seven days later. I don't know but what in their deepest hearts they don't want him to get off scot-free, get up to Liverpool and off on a boat. People feel like that, I don't know why. Robin Hood feeling.

And now it's a wonder how many people seem to know someone who's on the inside, inside the station, the copper's aunt lark. And it seems from these that this fellow Mortimer won't stop talking, they caution him but he makes statement after statement, and the long view is he's gone off his nut. They'll charge him, of course, but there's a lot never gets in the papers.

In a nutshell, he went for her with the chopper—it *was* a chopper—because *things were too good*. What about that?

It seems he sat down to his tea that night feeling all right, quite ordinary and normal, and then something comes over him, kind of a blackout, and he can't remember too much except for two things. One, he was sensible enough to take the kids out into the front room and turn the telly on, so he knew they'd stick there. Two, he seems to remember the general reason for what he did, though he wouldn't do it again in his right mind.

He said whenever he picked up a paper he saw a picture of himself and his missus and his kids. Never could he open a newspaper without seeing himself. There he was sitting up at the table, all smiling in a clean collar. Or looking round the kitchen door, smiling at his missus. Or smiling at the kids who were smiling. Or sometimes he wasn't there at all but only his missus smiling, or the kids smiling. All the family always in all the papers, pictures of them over the washtub or at the stove or sitting down at that great smiling white table.

Of course, it was the advertisements he was talking about. He'd look at his paper and see a smiling family there and then he'd look up slowly, just over the edge of the paper, and there sure enough was the same family smiling away fit to burst. It seems his wife's face was about the same as the kind of housewife they like to draw, and he had that clean big-jawed look, and the kids were just the type too.

So there it was. They were all too good to be true. So he made sure it wasn't true any more.

He'd sit in his cell, they said, and mumble. "Creamy, golden rich," he'd say to himself. "Get the outsize family size," he'd mutter. "It does you good!" he'd yell, "get it at *your* grocer!" And then he'd get worried about his plate when he'd had his grub—couldn't he help with the washing up, he'd ask, and the first time he tried to follow his plate out the door they thought he was trying to get out. He worried a bit about the home, too. Had he tidied up nicely, afterwards? He hadn't left a mess about?

It seemed, from what we heard, that he'd done about as nice a job of clearing up afterwards as the geezers at the Yard had ever seen.

He'd left the place spotless and it must have been a right sight. It makes you sorry for him—and for her—but you can't help but see him there in his little washing-up apron with the plastic frills getting the old detergent going—and they said each piece they found was wrapped up tidy in greaseproof paper, tied up

neat with string and a little loop to put your finger in
for carrying. It must have taken him quite a time. But
he was a useful handyman, keen on carpentry, a good
hand with a saw. He said it was a long job, but the
kids were in there with the telly and wild horses
wouldn't drag them away from *that,* they'd gone to
sleep peaceful as you please in the new telly-chairs
he'd got. He'd put them to bed upstairs and the next
morning took them out for a café breakfast, a real
treat. Then he'd telephoned his mother out at Eltham
that Ede, that was the deceased's name, had the 'flu
and could she take the kids in for a day or two, and
of course the old girl was only too glad to get her
hands on them and no questions asked, so down they
went by train that day early.

He cried about the kids sometimes, they said. But he
always seemed to cheer up. "Mum'll look after them,"
he said.

Poor devil, most of us thought, for somehow, what
with the way he'd seen to the kids, you felt he wasn't
so bad after all, he'd just come over very queer. But
there was one little fellow came up every evening and
stood outside the house on the other side of the road
looking at it and saying nothing, ginger-haired little
fellow with a kind of hungry look, and he'd come in the
Goat for a pint, and then go back and stand there looking. Hours he spent there, and never saying a word.
Made some of us a bit nervy—so finally the Governor
put it to him cheery-like: "And what brings you here,
my lord?" And then at last the little chap looks up, and
you felt there might be tears in his eyes so sorrowful he

looks, and he says just one word before he buries his puss in his pint again. "Envy," he says.

People were chipping bits off the front walls of the house—"souvenir" one of them protested right resentful at the copper who nabbed him. And one family opposite the Mortimers' in the gardens, next house along on our side, let the word around that anyone could go up for a look on a bob a quarter-hour basis. We expected the charrers any day.

Still—people in glass houses, me I couldn't keep my own eyes off and all the week it quite upset my viewing. I'd got the habit of borrowing old Mattie's binoculars to look over the house opposite, underneath Dawn's flat, where they had a telly showing every night. You could get in a good hour before they closed the curtains. But now where was the use, I'm forever switching over, one minute I'm mixed up with a good clean murder-play and the next we're down among the digging again, all among the mud and marrow where they're lighting matches and huddling over their torches like uncles on bonfire night—until they set up a little searchlight thing, when it looks like a wet deb-dance with no debs.

In the Goat they'd turned that picture of the bare two-legger in the lily-pond to the wall: all that charley wasn't nice any more, it gave the Green Howards chopper-eyes.

Old Mrs. Orme did more shopping per square inch of her three-and-six-an-hour than a duck's uncle. "I'm just going up the chemist's," she'd say, and saying it like that made her sound quite human for a change, and off she'd toddle to keep an eye on the door in Mather Street. And there was old Sir Hugh out on his scooter again putt-putting round the new police cars like a bubbling old boy scout—but he lost interest when he heard old Mortimer'd done it with the usual old chopper. He'd want something a little more progressive, would old Hughie, something like a bash on the nut with the home-espresso and the body whipped up in a launderette.

But Dawn—the funny thing about old Dawn was it scared the wits out of her, sobered her down proper! Know what she said? "It's going *too* far," she said. Honest. "Too much of a good thing," was what she whispered, touching wood with her eyes. Now, I'd've sworn she was the first for a bit of blood and thunder and a hairy hand in the night—but oh dear no, not when it's so near, not when it's next-door! Then old Mattie told me about the fight they had in the club and I caught on. It was simply that old Dawn was too near blue murder herself half the time, and this lot showed what happens when someone loses their head. It took the Queensberry out of her rules. She went about very straight-faced, if you can imagine such a thing.

But now about old Mattie. This was a very different kettle of fish. Mattie's trouble was double, or treble, treble trouble call it.

First, he can't help feeling about this murder, it's in the air and so is he and he can't get away from it. He'd like to. He'd like to rise right above it. The educated don't like to be upset, and what's even more they don't like to look it.

Secondly, he's up a gum-tree in any case—and all this doesn't keep the branches any steadier. I've never seen him like it with a two-legger and I've seen him around with half-a-dozen cool smashers in my time, and pretty bored he always looked . . . but this one . . . ! He's caught it nasty. And something else—you don't need a glass eye to see this Lily's gone for him just the same way. So it's all in the clear.

So what happens? So what does he do? Lovely old sod all. Nada. Nothing. Warms your heart, doesn't it?

You might suspect he was suspicious? Case of look-before-you-leap? No, it's more than that. It's because he's Mr. Clever and it's all too easy for Mr. Clever. Mr. Clever just *wants* to make it difficult. There you have it! Here's an ordinary man, not a raving nerve-case, nothing up the pole, an ordinary man looking like an ordinary man, a quiet but not too quiet one—like that you'd think it would be all fair sailing? Not on your bleeding life. These ordinary men are so damn compli-cated you could cry. "Oh Leslie I'm too old for her." "Oh Leslie you don't know how *remote* youth can be!" "Oh Leslie when I say Charley Cochran she won't know who I mean." Day in day out. "Oh Leslie, she'll want to stay up till all hours. And so she should, Leslie, so she should." This may be human nature, but to my mind its human nature *plus* education, and that's no bloody picnic.

Now that I've retired from the stage to become an

antiquarian, that is to say now my last walk-on was as far back as I don't like to think and I've taken to buying and selling a few useful and beautiful objects—I can see how simple life can be. It takes this kind of up-and-down life to keep you quiet inside—for where's the time left to get worried?—but just the opposite it takes a level, complete and quiet life to start the good old up-and-down inside. Like I live, you haven't time. Humping ice-cream on the night-line, taking the old pole round the gas-lamps, sitting around with babies or digging graves up the boneyard for three bob an hour—which is about as near to Yorick as I'll ever be—there's an actor's life for you, telly or no telly, and you haven't time to add to life's abundant complications. But give us a private income, give us old Mattie's good looks and a bit of a brain, give us the time and the money and you'd think things would be a little easier, wouldn't you? I'll say.

However—what now happens to our blue-eyed boy, our child of good fortune but exactly what he wants? Trouble.

In a word, Dawn. It seems old Dawn is not so scared by the chopping that she can't get up to a few tricks too. It appears Mattie has offered Lily a job and Dawn hears of it and it is not at all to her liking, oh by no means no. It appears the Misses Lily and Dawn have quite a show-down between themselves. Dawn wants her sis at the Acacia, being a good investment and sisterly too, two birds a stone, yet despite this heaven-sent opportunity to lift her up into the gutter, which many girls would give their wellingtons for—Miss Lily thinks she'd like a breath of fresh air. And of course it's not just any job, it's a job of Mr. Ligne's, the hook on the end of the Ligne heigh-ho. And Dawn sees more in this than meets her eye.

And Dawn is no simple girl. She's not green and she doesn't like the feel of grass shyly peeping underfoot. So since she's mad at Mattie, what does she do? Makes up she's mad *for* him, of course. Drops the pearl-handled look and makes a bee-line for the old boy's heart and whatever other parts of him might be privately available. In this of course, her judgment's all to hell. She doesn't see—or she doesn't like to see—that he's not after Lily in any common or garden way. And anyhow, what woman likes to think she can't do the trick if she puts her mind to it, if you could call it a mind, if you could call it a woman?

Poor old Matthew doesn't see what's coming. Since he's wanting things more complicated, he's naturally trying to smooth them out, Dawn in particular—so when she rings him up and asks him up for a drink with her, up goes my lord like a lamb. And a couple of drinks and ten minute's guff and old Dawn's got her old arms round about him. And a gentleman like my lord can't quite throw a lady off, this being rude. And of course Dawn knowing the right time, Lily comes in and finds them at it. End of Act I Scene II.

I had real trouble with him next day. Ordinarily I could get his mind off things a bit. Get him to look at the telly through the operas, ask him which pussy he thought dug up Mrs. Mortimer, or something. But after Lily finds him with Dawn it's no go, no go nothing at all. Mattie's had it, good and true, the balloon's gone up and it's every man for himself. And why? Because Lily bawls him out? Not on your life. Oh no, it's much more complicated than that for Mr. Clever.

Matthew, standing in Dawn's rose-curtained room, now lit not by nightlight but by the dying sun's buff rays shed through lace to gild the rose in the room with a dull dead sadness—such light as he knew from sea-side bedrooms, pink curtains faded in the salt air, the end of the day and outside a white balcony fretting over wet deserted sands—Matthew, as this sad sun picked out on a mantle a little china cupid whose arms surrounded a gold clock, was startled to see the round pink biceps of Dawn's own sleeveless arms go round him and to feel her whole rubber-bound body bump into his.

From beneath her hair beneath his eyes her voice came mumbling clearly, " . . . d'you know I go for you, I've tried to stop myself, I've even acted sore but I couldn't be sore with you Ligney, Ligney *darling* not for long I couldn't be sore, because I go for you, Ligney, I can't stop myself. . . . "

And all the time her arms were tightening on him and her hands fixing into his back, and suddenly she threw her head right back so that her hair tossed out a wide pink halo and she gave him her full huge face with a great straight stare, mouth wide and big blue lids lowered right down.

As his own arms still hung doing nothing, simply

clasped at attention in hers, two startled thoughts like bad birds flew in to shock him. One, that she had been, or could still by some be called, attractive: coarse indeed, as a loud lewd close-up printed in big dots in a newspaper—but it appalled him that he should notice this. And secondly a dreadful and automatic echo came from the past, a terrible feeling of success—that here was another one in his arms and chalk it up, boy. Both thoughts passed instantly, parts of a shudder, and he was left only with nausea and trapped horror growing huge like a tree, filling the room with panic shadow, stifling as the chypre rising round her like a light, mind-clouding gas. Traffic cries from the outside street seemed ever further and freer away. He could not stiffen himself more. Nor raise his arms. Nor take them away. But what was more fearful than all this was that here stood a woman speaking out her heart, offering her body—and it would be rough, rude, impolite, unchivalrous and cruel to make any harsh movement of rejection. Besides—and the calculation occurred to him even in that mixed and fearful moment—a woman scorned would be furious as hell. Dawn must be retained at least as a neutral, if not an ally.

His mind shot blindly for excuse. And he began to cough. He began to pretend a fit of coughing, doubling himself up in her arms, hoping she would not think he was choking with laughter—but this could not have been so, for what she did was hit him sharply on the back with both fists already there, thus loosening neither arms nor body but tightening the clasp of both in such emergency.

"Oh, has something gone down the wrong way?"
she laughed hitting him, and he felt the soft splay of her
big bosom flattened onto him and further down num-
berless hard knots and little corset girders as the machinery of her underdress bit into him. But hands
pinioned to his side he could not cover his mouth—
and so as she hit him he raised his head and coughed
straight into her open face before turning sharply aside
like a soldier eyes-righting the Colours.

The Colours were a long gold-framed looking-glass
in which he saw the whole blue body of her, from her
tousled pink hair to her very beautiful legs with now
not butterflies but notes of music playing round the
seams, and as all this high-heeled at him, he coughed:
"Please . . . I must . . . get rid. . . . "

"Poor sweet," she cooed, but never letting him go led
him to the big cushion-piled divan bed, and he had to
let himself be led, only hoping when he sat down he
could somehow free himself. But once down she put
her head on his chest again, and now he saw a yellow-
grey break in her pink hair where it parted and the
rough powdered pinkness of a side of cheek and then
realized her lips would be on his white collar smearing
lipstick—and somehow this gave him the practical excuse of keeping clothes clean and he prised his arms
up and at last, gently, firmly, began to push her away.

Just as the door opened and Lily with a parcel came
in.

Lily stood for a moment isolated, and his heart
screamed for shadow to hide in but the setting sun

seemed to light up every laced, gilded, pink-hung corner of the room.

And—now his arms were up, half-freed, as if he too
were embracing! Lipstick on his collar! Dawn's hair
tousled and upset! Old stories of men accused falsely
of assault in railway carriages flew through his mind:
but there was no five-minute ash on his cigar to prove
he had sat still, and the man is always held to blame,
even to-day they still equate woman with modesty,
there was no doubt but any explanation he could try
to make would sound weak and absurd—and how in
any case to put it into words? He sprang up. Dawn
lazed back, stretching herself like a huge blue cat, a
cat with the face of a kind of baby hippopotamus, and
dropped words viscous and slow as red treacle: "Hello,
darling? Sweet of you to knock."

Lily only slyly smiled. "Well Matthew," she said,
"doing the rounds?"

He heard his voice strained and sharp. "Lily, this has
got to be explained—"

"Don't bother."

She walked across the room and he watched her grey
and slender against the weak sunglare as she put down
her parcel carefully on a table.

"But I *must* explain. Lily, *please*—"

"Do-o-o-n't bother." Now she was lightly mocking
in a kind of staged voice.

"Ligney and I," said Dawn from deep in her throat,
stroking the words, "were just having a little drink. . . ."

"So I see," said Lily brightly. "I'll bet you two were
right thirsty."

"Lily, *please* let me—" He hated to see her behave so brightly, like a cheerless little heroine in a cheap film.

But Lily interrupted him and said calmly: "I did say don't bother and I meant it. She's only up to her tricks again and I know them all too well and nothing will ever teach her."

Now he saw she was smiling quite naturally at him, she had never played coy at all, nor gaily petulant nor anything, she was simply and truly disregarding the whole affair.

But it upset Dawn. "What tricks?" she shouted jumping up and walking about pulling her corset straight. "What tricks? I ask him up socially and he makes a grab at me."

Lily turned her eyes to the ceiling and sighed. She took her time lighting a cigarette.

"Oh for heaven's sake—" Matthew began.

But Dawn went on straight at Lily's face. "What could I do alone here?" she started, "I had to take it, as you for one well know you've got to when you're alone with a fellow. Don't you now?"

Lily put her cigarette down. "That's enough."

She turned to Matthew. "That's not true, you know."

Matthew nodded. There was no question of not believing her.

Dawn's face gave a wry sideways smile, shiftily defeated. She shrugged and said nothing. The room subsided into its air of dead gold sunset, dismal and dull. There seemed nothing more to be said. Matthew's mind began to race against the awkward indifference of the room, too slow now—so he said he had better go, and after a moment left. But as he went through the door Lily spoke again: "I'd like to take that job," she said, "by the way."

By the way? What did that mean? And why had she decided on the job—as a simple move against Dawn? Or was it something else, double-talk, some intricate message to him?

Half an hour later his mind was still racing. It raced as he thought of the immediate dispassion with which she had seen through Dawn's embrace of him. Right there in the room! It raced at the efficiency with which she had instantly swept away such an obstacle. For here had been the makings of a fine misunderstanding between them, something at last for him to fight against and overcome—and phut! she had blown it over with a glance. And again the way was clear. Again there were no difficulties, she was there ready and willing for him, and again he felt that this must be all wrong.

He sat in his room knowing how he must act, waiting somehow for his brain to give permission to his mind to begin. He was exactly like a diver on the end of the high diving-board, a diver who has climbed there because he wants to, and who now surveys the air and the water through which he wishes to dive, who sees there is no obstacle between himself and his desire—yet still hesitates.

That diver would not hesitate if someone gave him a push. Nor if perhaps a wind came from behind— enough to make him shiver. Nor, it is quite likely, if something occurred perhaps miles away—a steamer sounding its siren, a bugle suddenly calling: even such far-away excitements might be enough to set initiative into motion.

And something very like this, a massing of many indirect forces, occurred then in Matthew's suspended life. There he was, he thought, come away from exactly the place he wanted to be—over the gardens in that house opposite where Lily was. It was about six o'clock. The whole intolerable evening stretched ahead. He had lost all his adult ability to use the empty hours —the kind of patience that sees the end of them, the same patience that kicks back on the elderly making time seem always to fly, their sense of impatience at fault. The years fell from him, he felt like a clerk with a clock, a boy with the weeks of term, a young man and a penniless evening.

He could not see how he could get through the hours without her. He saw each quarter and half hour dwindle round the clock, saw dinner waiting and the food to be swallowed not tasted, and then, that over, more hours ahead in the darkness when lamps would be lit and others everywhere settle down for their evening's purpose . . . but he?

That sunset above the roofs opposite made a wild and golden desolation of the sky, small clouds with a glitter of plush floated on a westering watery sea painted peacock and rose and furnaced orange, the whole sky was ablaze with the bright melancholy of London's soot-black chimneys and smoke-laden trees, evening of the giant sad city watching another spring day die. Such sunsets disturb, and now from somewhere in the well of houses came the sound of a piano slowly playing a sad old dance-tune, a belling memory of bars and dances, echoing all moments lost at dances in youth, all lost moments of dying days . . . and then from somewhere else a voice laughed, loud and clear . . . and he was looking over at her window still dark because she must be still in the front of the house with Dawn, her window dead without her.

They were still digging in the Mortimers' garden. He noticed that the well-dressed man who owned the paved, treeless garden next door was out pacing and peering and smiling, smoking a cigarette: he recalled now vaguely that when the night before he had put out the pussies' food in the garden he had seen what he had thought to be the night-lit eye of a one-eyed cat slither along the wall—it must have been this man's quiet-gliding cigarette end.

People were still on the watch, he thought. And then suddenly the sky changed from gold to green, a bright green light fired his windows and this was reflected by those opposite—so that for a moment he thought there was a light in Lily's room—and the piano played louder and suddenly all the constrained excitement of the past days since the murder rose to a head in him, all the whispering and crowding and peering that he had tried to overlook took its proper charge, he who was full of his own excitement realized suddenly how much of this other tense atmosphere he had repressed, it had been working at him all the time, everyone around the gardens had been living a little faster, a nervous infection had bred its epidemic air, it was like all other moments when difficulties stir up massed emotions—times of

fierce winter weather, strikes, coronations, bombard-
ment—and a general excitement stimulates private action. Repose had taken a holiday, the disturbance was
absolute, and suddenly he felt he must act or break.

Voices sounded abruptly from the laurel-dripping
garden to his right, where properly a body should have
been found. That man in the tweed overcoat, evidently
a prospective purchaser of the house, had called again,
but with a different man in a mackintosh. It was this
last man's voice that now rose passionately as a boot
kicked away at mouldered plaster: "Look at it! *Look*
at it! Lousey with damp. I wouldn't want a pig to live
here, honest I wouldn't.

"Look at those sashes!" he said. "Look at that paint,
botched as my ruddy grandmother, good lord it *hurts*.

"Oh no," he wailed, shaking his head from side to
side, "oooh no, I don't like it, honest I don't." He leaned
forward and with his naked hand broke off a consider-
able piece of the house. The tweed-coated man coughed
uncomfortably. Who would be responsible? This man
was indeed his surveyor but how could he know the
passionate hatred of a surveyor for a house when his
blood is roused?

Matthew looking down remembered the flattering
voices of the agents a few days before, how they had
caressed the house, voices from similar mackintoshes.
How different two sides of a question could be! Who
was to believe anything? Presumably not the tweeded
gentleman. And how about the jury investigating poor
Mr. Mortimer? And how about himself?

Suddenly he thought that if Lily took that job it

would remove her from the window—and then the gathering of all these events burst in him, and as it burst he felt instantly freer, a breath of good air filled him and he picked up the telephone. Yes, she would meet him in a quarter of an hour. Yes, as usual, yes.

He took her firmly past the pub where they sometimes drank and began to walk her round a large neighbouring square. On foot, strolling the spring evening, they would not be disturbed.

First he had to ask about Dawn. Was she mad at them? In any case what had come over the woman, that is, with regard to him?

"That's simple," Lily said in her off-hand, simple way. "She heard about the job and she hates you anyway so the obvious thing was to pretend to be in love with you."

"Does that follow?"

"Since she hates you, she thought you hated her."

"Oh."

"And this was the best way of winning you over. I was really incidental—my intrusion, I mean."

"But she never thought I would—"

"Why not? She has quite an opinion of herself."

"Good lord."

"She's in a right good temper now," Lily said, "behaving like a naughty little girl. Found out. Hitting back."

"Little girl. Good lord."

"You'll have to be rather nice to her, I think. I don't

mean nice in a nasty way. Just nice. It'll be all the more
peaceful all round."

"Lily?"

"Yes?"

They were coming out from the older part of the
square where gaslamps fluttered among new leaves and
old stucco houses, and into a newer side made up of a
single great block of dark red Edwardian flats. The
pavements here were lit by yellow fog-lighting from
tall concrete standards. Nevertheless, as his lips turned
black and a red pillar box turned khaki, he took her
arm and continued:

"Lily, the other night when I offered you that job I
was going to say something quite different. Only something else—not only that beastly cat—stopped me. I
suppose that something else was the question of our
ages, the difference, and perhaps the fact that we don't
really know each other very well; I mean, we've only
just met, haven't we?"

"Yes."

"I was going to propose to you, my darling, and
that's, well, that's what I'm doing now."

"Yes."

"What."

"I said yes."

"I mean, I'm proposing marriage, Lily."

"Yes."

"Oh—you mean—?"

She said nothing.

"But I want to say so much first, Lily, because here
I am, getting on for forty I suppose, I'm thirty-nine, and

you're only twenty-one. That's eighteen years difference. And I should think it's an important eighteen
years, particularly for you, you're young and the next
eighteen years is going to be the most important part
of your life. I don't see it's right to ask you to share
that with me. I've lived through that time myself, and
I suppose I'm due to settle down a bit. And another
thing, I'm not all that well, I don't know which way
this stomach trouble's going, perhaps it's nothing, but
equally it might make me into an old dodderer before
my time."

He pulled a face to belittle this, and looked down.
But she was staring straight ahead, her face drawn
in the yellow fogflare. He was startled, seeing her suddenly so ill, but then saw what it was—and it occurred
to him how whole romances must nowadays be con-
ducted in such nightlight, there must be young men
who had never kissed red lips, only black.

He laughed, he was elated, a sense of action filled
him and kept him talking, telling her all he had wanted
to for so long, putting the case carefully, as it should
be put, fairly to her and clearly to himself. That part
of his character which had made him able in business
management had been set working.

"But on the other hand," he went on, "if you're going
to spend those next eighteen years jazzing about the
Acacia Room, I don't see that's going to do you much
good either. I mean, it doesn't make what I have to
offer so much out of balance. That kind of life's all very
well at first. I can see it's exciting. I mean, after the
country, after Flint. But heaven knows what it'll do to

you as time goes on, what's it going to do to you in the end?"

She spoke at last then: "A lost woman?"

He coughed at this: "Well, no I didn't mean . . . not exactly. . . . "

"But you mean, exactly, that you're rescuing me?"

He laughed: "No, no, of course not. I just meant, that sort of life's—" He finished this with a gesture of his free arm, and heard her laugh too. He hugged her arm closer to him, and felt her hand grip his hand, and they walked on, now out of the yellow light towards the green and the gas again. Older houses. Wistaria-hung Trafalgar balconies. In between, a sudden square modern house, a cross between a beach-hut and a little transformer station.

"Now darling you know very little about me," he went on. "But I can give you at least the bare bones such as the house is mine and there's seven hundred a year of my own and I kick up another two or three thousand, good years more, at this business of running businesses."

He went on, telling her everything he could about his mother and Leslie and what the doctors had said about his stomach. He told her concisely, as quickly and plainly as he could to get it said, now and forever, before she could say "yes."

It took them once round the square again, back into the yellow and back into the green gas once so garish but soft as candlelight against the modern glare—and he welcomed this as lucky that they should have come round to this quieter, older, more romantic side of the square as finally he came to a stop, and stopped their walking, and faced her and put his arms round her to look her full and straight in the eyes, and said:

"Lily, my love, will you marry me?"

The old gaslamps among spring leaves seemed to waver in the silence. Far away, the slight hum of traffic. Above, a sky richening with the rose reflection of London's lights.

"No," she said.

Sounds broke out everywhere. The quiet had been of his own making. He had shut his ears in towards her. Now they were broken wide open. A car swished by, its lights for a second showing clearly her upturned face with eyes looking past him and over his shoulder.

"What?" he stammered.

"No," she said. "I'm sorry, Matthew—but no."

"Oh."

He realized his hands were on her, and felt he ought to take them off. He let them drop to his sides, he did not know what to do or say so he put one of them in a pocket and half-turned away. At length, "I'm sorry," he said. "I somehow thought—stupid, after the other other night and you did say—"

"I said a lot and I meant a lot," she said. "But . . . no, Matthew."

He felt huge and spare, a big body with nothing inside him, inflated and empty: and now with a kind of petulance asked: "What did you expect me to do?"

It was awkward to stand edging opposite each other, and they started strolling again. But now to Matthew, as she began to speak, it seemed to be that the square moved round them, like a picture on a roll, he felt so much stuck back at the spot where she had said No.

"I suppose you might say I've been leading you on," she said, "I suppose that's so in a way. I thought we could be good friends. Of course that's absurd, one always goes further—but how far I don't know, you don't gauge these things, and I dare say now I'm, I was, no I *am*, a little in love with you." Her head was bowed, she was speaking to the pavement coming towards them, her voice too calm and considerate, as if she were counting the pavement cracks. It was a hard and small voice. They were no longer arm-in-arm.

"Then I'm new to London, it was fun to find someone I liked to go around with. And I wanted to get away—I know it's horrid to say so, from Dawn—and I suppose you fitted in and why shouldn't I have a good time—" her voice rose then, a single unbalanced sob broke it, and then: "Oh damn . . . I can't explain . . . let me go. . . ."

And she turned abruptly and walked away, a lonely figure head down in the lamplight, loneliness in the hurry of her quick footsteps.

But then as suddenly stopped. And turned back. Just then strip-lighting flickered, snapped hard and violet through pale slatted blinds in the modern house by which they now stood. Her voice was quieter as she said: "I'm sorry. It was really nice of you to tell me all that so carefully. Perhaps that made me see clearly why it would be wrong."

She peered up at him: he felt suddenly that she expected him to say something. The violet light drained her cheeks white, but shadowed her eyes softer, darker. They seemed to be asking something.

"I don't see what I can say," he said. "I'll try to understand."

As at any other moment of parting, there was an impulse to embrace: he felt his hands move towards her, he wanted terribly to kiss her face, to love against it with his—but his hands stopped and his eyes went down to the little space between them. He felt hopelessly formal. It was forbidden.

But they would have to take the same direction home? Walk together in silence? So it came to him to say: "I'm going to have a drink," and it felt boorish not to ask her.

"Then I'd better go," she said, as if this place on the pavement where so much had been said was where he lived. She turned and walked away, no longer hurrying, slowly and tired.

He watched her go, still standing on his square of pavement. He could scarcely bear the fact that she was alone, no one at all at her side.

Then she turned the corner, and was gone.

He turned the other way. He walked slowly away from home. A cat stepped out from bushes into the light and looked at him dangerously, ears back, alert. He did what he never did, flapped at it with his hand. The cat slipped off like a shadow close down, and he walked on feeling worse than ever.

Suddenly he remembered how her lonely figure going away was not to be lonely for long—she was only beginning the evening. At a time when—surely?—one should be quietly alone to think—there was a whole evening of music and lights and people to face! It did not bear thinking of. Nothing bore thinking of. He walked on, feeling a lump grow in his throat and the wet feeling swell at his eyelids; then pulled himself together, walked faster towards no destination, felt this and slowed impatiently down—for what purpose was there in doing anything, going fast or slow or anywhere? He took the ordinary course, and turned into the first saloon bar. He had a stiff drink and it did a little good.

The hours ahead, simply the hours of this one evening, extended themselves blank and unbearable. He tried to concentrate on one practical aspect. What, for instance, about that job? He resolved to fix it by letter.

The distance between them was suddenly so great that even this thought was possible: Had he tricked himself? Had he really wanted her? And then through all the desolation, the lonely base vacuity, a kind of excitement purred deep in the back of his mind. For at last there was an obstacle, insurmountable indeed but nevertheless an obstacle, and provided by herself, neither by misunderstanding nor by circumstances, but purely from her own lips. In a way he loved her for it.

TWELVE

WELL NOW, Leslie said, this is where we came in, and
the lord-and-master back at his window like a cat on
cold bricks, prowling fit to make you weep, miaou,
miaou.

His girl done him wrong. He starts changing the
rooms about again; a black look from Lily, and me and
old Orme drop everything to hump furniture. We're
getting used to it. He's already had me out of my old
room above, put me in the front, and now it's all his
books to the front again and me back to the top back.
On top of which he's still back in his bottom back half
the day—"Just having a look down the gardens, Les."—
"Can't think where the *Statesman's* got to." "Leslie, did
you hear a noise? Sounded like a cat." What cat? Lily
the Cat.

You'd think he was an old peep-bo tomming the
sights again, safely stuck behind his curtain with a
nice book handy. But that's not Ligne's line, you could
have stripped the Queen of Sheba and thrown in Shef-
field Thursday and he wouldn't have looked that-a-
way. I knew a man once who took *bricks out of a wall*

for this purpose, and God knows how many little round knots of wood are knocking about the world with no place to go. But not Matthew. Not that I blame him, you never see much, they get you nicely on your toes then reach for the curtains casual, like an afterthought. Sometimes I think there's a conspiracy about. I know a chap went to Marseilles for a bit of fun, no harm done, man of the world, and where does he go but to the local spectacle and what does he see? The Dagenham Girl Pipers. That's the Saturday. On the Monday he flies to Algiers. That week they have a speciality there—Les Dagenham. Back to Barcelona? Las Dagenhamas. Followed him half-way round the world, those girls did. Very nice too, but he's never been the same.

No, you've got to be a window-cleaner to do the job properly, and a proper job they do from what they tell me, what with hubby at the office and the missus handing out cups of you and me with plenty of me. Home life isn't all telly, not by a long way. I know a nice young chap in the electrical line, didn't like his cup of tea, really *wanted* to mend the vacuum and what does this mother-of-three do but get him the sack! Cheeked her, she said. Sweet old lady.

However, Matthew. Matthew makes out he's looking for a book or heard a cat or looking the Mortimers' way—but half an eye can see different to that last one; the party's over, the digging's done, and the next thing we'll hear is poor old Mortimer's doing a little gardening up Broadmoor way.

Which upsets the old Goat as much as my Matthew. Dumb as oxes, they're knocked groggy by it all, nothing to talk about now it's over. There's only one bit of news comes in cheers them up a bit—it seems he's begun to kick up hell about his garden. Caught on to how they had to dig up the pieces. "What they been doing to my beans?" he hollers. "What's my marrows like?" Doesn't trust them an inch. Seems he put the parcels in carefully so as not to disturb the roots. And now what? Bogeys! With *spades!*

Then there's also the trick-cyclist who comes to see him and says the case is quite simple. Mortimer is like a child building a house neat and lovely with his bricks, brick upon brick upon brick till it's done and it's the most beautiful house in all the whole wide world and he's made it himself and it's *his.* So what does he do, this happy nipper? Gets the needle and knocks it all down, of course. It's a common feeling, this cyclist says. Man and perfection don't mix, he says. Arrival, he says, is but another point of departure. And so all the geezers in the Goat look down at theirselves to see if they haven't arrived, and thank their lucky stars to see they haven't, at least they can be sure of *that* one.

But the best of all is the Press. They can't get much, having to wait for the trial and so on, but what they serve up slays us stone cold: "It is understood," write the gentlemen of the Press, "that the deceased was planning to leave the country for the Argentine." Heigh-ho.

So you'd think, all in all, it would be a pretty slow time?

Not for long you wouldn't. When things go slow we don't believe it, do we? We get our weather-eye out.

We know life'll be upside down again by the end of the week—all we need do is just hold on and something or other'll blow the works, there's nothing settled about *this* life, like four days later when I meet Mattie on the front steps carrying a toy bow-and-arrows, a Sioux Set I see from the box, and I think that's better, he's gone out and got a present for some kid and that shows a bit of interest at least.

Not a bit of it. When I go upstairs a quarter-hour later he's got the whole blooming shooting match out, there's arrows sticking all over the wall, and here's my lord-and-master propped up in his chair twanging away like Big Chief Running Water in person. Well, it's no business of mine if he wants to spend the night shooting up his bottle damask flock at six-pound-a-piece— except he nearly throws a fit when I come in. I get the big flea: "Why can't you *knock*, Leslie? Can't you see I'm busy, man? Can't a fellow have a moment's peace?" *Peace*. Natch, I don't like the look of things. What with Mortimer gone off his nut, you never know.

And I'm not far wrong. That very afternoon, it's the Wednesday and I won't ever forget it, down the stairs he comes hollering: "Ambulance! Ambulance!" he hollers and "Lily! quick!" and gallops off flying down the steps and round the corner to Mather.

So there I am on the blower to nine nine nine. Having a slow time.

The morning after Lily had refused him, Ligne sat in his front room again and thought: it's all finished.

But since he also sat there thinking of himself thinking it, did he quite believe it? And what should he, or could he, do about it? He wavered between two attitudes—a proper civility that if she had said no then she had meant no and her conviction must be respected: the other involved a more human humanity, to try by any and every means to make her change her mind. The former, as much self-protective as civilized, prevailed.

He looked out on the passing street, and transferred his dejection to the heads bobbing past. A city of people bowed by acquisition directions, hurrying, struggling, pointless—their only repose the alcoholic ounce, the grain of salicylic acid. What a procession of deceptive buoyancies—limbs of the present dragged on by eyes on the future! But to have no future makes the present taste sweeter? He had heard that one before.

Then along the street there shot a giant toothpaste tube, it's driver huddled somewhere in the cap. Matthew shuddered, pretended that he could bear such a street no longer, and wandered malingering out into the passage and into his old room.

For once he went straight up to the window, making no attempt to disguise himself. What would be the point? Let her see him alone and dejected, let it strike her conscience and to hell with courtesy . . . but a moment later he was retreated again behind the curtain. Such a display would be unfair to her! It was also a little too dramatic for his own comfort.

But no movement at the window opposite. And down in the Mortimers' the digging was over. All the people of the gardens, as if exhausted by so much excitement, had crept into their shells. It was a dull day, the sky quite white. Only the cats were out. Dupont sat washing his behind with one leg stuck high like an upholstered beer-pull: turned in on himself, like the day.

Like a child on a rainy afternoon, he took in the machinery of the window close to his eye—screws and pulley-wheels painted over; sashcords; the window catch funnelled like a squat brass puffer; a fat bluebottle, hairy with legs, dead on its back: desolation everywhere. That piano was playing again—now the same music that had sounded so evocatic tinned dully on the dull dead air.

He tried a book, then a paper—put both down and returned to his stand between the curtains. All the time those words of Lily's repeated themselves. It appalled him that after so short a time he could not remember all she had said. Isolated sentences volleyed at him out of the mist. "It was fun to find someone to go around with." Fun! *Fun!* And then: "One always goes further." How did she know? Did she, had she? And how far was further? The words grew huge and he tried both to make the best and the worst of them, equally. He remembered how hard her voice had been, she had said hard things without seeming to care. Had she tricked him all along? He thought back to that moment in the graveyard and again the feeling of double-talk came confounding him: she had been shaking with laughter.

Now he would never be with her again. But he would see her from this window. However many rooms

he changed he would be back watching and torment-
ing himself. I must get away, he thought, clamping
himself harder to the sill.

He went down to a gloomy lunch with Leslie. Then
returned to wander about the rooms, always ending
back by that window. He forced himself out for a walk
—and after an hour's self-pity in the park, again returned. No tree, statue, dog or person had seemed to
have any point. It was best to be alone.

Now it was after four o'clock and there were dim
stirrings in the dark windows, afternoon rests were
done, tea was being made. He thought of the pieces of
Mrs. Mortimer buried neatly about the garden soil—
and looking up at all the rows of windows suddenly
saw how all the people there took themselves to pieces
each night—he saw dentures coming out, chignons off,
corsets unpoppered, stays unlaced; he saw the shedding
of built-up shoes and neck-stiffening collars, shoulder-
pads, foam-rubber breastlets and all the rest of this
secret assembly-line of the bedroom. There, dead opposite, it happened behind the backs of those dressing-
tables from which so busily now an arm, now a
shoulder protruded . . . and *what*, he screamed to himself, what *for*?

For the many interests and purposes of their many
lives. From which he was excluded.

Everybody but himself in these houses had a purpose
and a direction. The great exclusion of cities closed
over him—the momentary glimpses of people in cars,
through windows, in shops, on the street, purposeful
people all dressed up and somewhere to go, seen once

and never seen again, vanished forever, curtains drawn.

No longer did he see the alcohol and aspirin drones of the morning—his thoughts were swinging quite wildly.

When the sun shone, he felt a little better, as if life had somewhere a crude importance. Lily never appeared at the window. He wondered whether she had gone away. He considered going to the Acacia Room to find out. To telephone was unthinkable—he could not manage the quiet click of cowardice as, no word spoken, the receiver must be replaced. He thought of standing on the street corner to watch if she went out: but experience reminded him what a shuffling, secretive, embarrassed time the street corner would mean. So he stayed in. He did not want to be alone and he did not want to be with people. People would take him out of himself. Did he want to be taken out of himself? Neither. Nothing would do. He wanted to lose himself in a book, or music, or even the wireless—but soon stopped troubling even to cross the room to any one of these, just sat and looked at the bookcase, the gramophone horn, the wireless, rejecting them from where he sat.

And one day—two, three days later?—, and when he was not looking, the curtains across the way were drawn to and a light turned on. She was there, behind the curtains, fifty yards away. She would be doing things, moving about the room! Reading her "old hat" Baudelaire? Undressing—and in his imagination her back was turned and she wore a dressing-gown—for a bath? Or answering the telephone? Who was calling,

Sanderson? But on the whole he drew comfort from the simple fact that she was *there*.

But she never appeared by day. Was this some consideration for him? Or conscience about him? Or even some kind of unhappiness? On the other hand she might just be out—having this "fun" she specialized in?

Her window gaped like an empty stand in a full shop window. Miss Tigerpants still hurried around her room with parcels and baskets, slowing down as she passed her mirror, accelerating afterwards like a car passing a crossing: Jacko was still seen carrying his bicycle upstairs and downstairs—he even acted the toiler alone by himself, rubbing a dramatic hand across his brow to sweep off honest, unseen sweat. Mrs. Peabasin had another lady to tea, they sat nearly indistinguishable in dark blue dresses and there was no shelling that day. The bald-headed roseman had laid his garden with fertilizer, and a smell of bad wet Bombay Duck hung about the air. Next door that man in the tweed coat must finally have bought the house— for there were workmen in all manner of rough clothes walking about the garden as brutally as a master-race: strange, too, in a mechanized world to see such grown men carrying buckets of sand and throwing bricks to one another. Mrs. Mortimer's garden lay deserted: yet the earth which had so recently covered her remains still lay untidily turned up—at least they might have raked it back. A few houses down a man walked about the roof, an enormous figure against the sky, dwarfing the chimneys.

And what did he himself look like to that man, to all

the others? Everybody lives in two houses—the one they imagine and the one that visitors see. How did they see him, standing up in his own chequer board of sashes and brick? A grey shadow at the window? The lonely one pressed against the pane, the Rain Man?

Then one afternoon the sky grew suddenly dark, white plaster flashed against the lowering grey above —he was reminded of that black shower a month ago when Lily had leaned out of the window and laughed among the hailstones—and now, at three o'clock, he had to switch on the light. Instantly the gardens outside turned to blue shadow—and suddenly he saw himself and his lampshade projected far out towards her window, a gold-lit ghost yearning towards her. Suppose she too switched on her light! Would the two ghosts, unseen by each other, meet in limbo above the gardens, in garden air touching between the houses?

Glass! Abruptly his nerves broke into a hundred sharp screeching fragments of glass. All these days he had been inside glass, glass, glass—glass never clear, glass dust-beamed, glass rain-dropped, glass breath-fogged, glass alive with flecks of old paint livering up the eyes. . . . How with glass can you say you see what you see? Airliners flap like ancient lizard-birds, wings waved in a fault in the glass. All flicker and fuss—and what is it made of anyway? Sand! Sand, sand *sand* in your eyes! Bulb-flash in the electric dusk, sunflash as the evening turns green, trees glassed darkly on the window in noonshine stiller than the moon's, yet all on a summer day—what frosting of the senses goes with glass you can't smell through, deaf glass where no air breaths?

Frangible, fractured, refracted, reflected . . . but on reflection, his light-bulb was only a few feet, a long jump, out in the garden air . . . and, sighing, the sharp and dancing mood declined, it had only screeched high for a moment. Now quietened, he reached out a hand to switch the grey daylight back again. As the switch clicked, the gardens came into being instantly. But they were not quite the same. The grey now had an edge, like a steel engraving, coldly exciting.

In fact, this small nervous outburst jerked life into him. As a few days before he had been stirred into action by a restlessness in the air, now he was stimulated by its exact opposite, he was galvanized by dullness.

His first impulse was to act against her, to go out and have a good dinner, get joyfully drunk, go to bed with a woman or two. His hand reached for the telephone— but stopped as an unusual idea came to him. This was, to go out and buy something he had seen in a toy shop, a set of bow-and-arrows. Injuns, he thought with sudden delight. The ritual round of dinner, drink, women receded—he was filled with the wish to do something childish and really irresponsible. It was the same freedom, on a wilder level, that invests the hand that reaches for the glass that contains the hangover, and what the hell? Off the rails—that was the place to be!

So Matthew, a man in a single-breasted blue suit, a leaseholder stepping from his adult house, keys jingling in his pockets, went off down the street to the toy shop to buy a bow-and-arrows. Inside the blue casing, his blood bubbled with delight. Inside his waist-coat, his heart danced the hop-skip-and-a-jump of a bishop alone with four reproachless walls.

He stood for a moment at the window, selecting be-tween a Sioux Set and "The Scalp-Hunter—do it the Ojibway," with which was included a tomahawk. "Not a tomahawk," Matthew said to himself, "Mortimer re-quiescat," he bubbled. To the left of the Sioux Set stood a blue-bonnetted girl-elephant with her trunk tied in a knot—*Little Forget-me-knot (Friction Drive)*: to the right there were dispersed a number of small lead figures caught in the First Position and marked *Unbreakable Ballet Dancers*. Matthew paid quickly and left.

He met Leslie on the way into the house, and in a moment his chuckling turned to a snigger. Discovered! But he said nothing, left Leslie to cock an eyebrow all to himself, and went on up the stairs, shut the door of his room, and felt secure again. He unpacked the bow, fixed an arrow and sent it whizzing into the wall. It stuck there with a quick little shiver. He nodded ap-proval. Then he sat himself at leisure in the big club chair and shot the whole quiverful into the wall. He aimed at a selected swirl in the wallpaper pattern. Soon, after collecting the arrows and trying again and again, he became more practised, and hit the mark more than once.

He never questioned these new high spirits. They were part of a game, a private game, a clever game, yes even a gambit, for they were constructive, they concerned Lily—the only thing that worried him was whether the bow might not be strong enough. He spent some time restringing it: it was a formidable weapon in any case, terrible for a toy shop.

When Leslie came in without knocking, it was precisely this problem that filled his mind: he told Leslie off less from fear of discovery than because the matter was accelerating and he could not bear interference. And when Leslie had gone he hurried to his desk and tore sheets of writing paper into quarters. On each of these he wrote a message.

Then he fixed the little squares of paper round the heads of the arrows, folded them neatly back to allow for a proper airflow, and opened the window.

Lily's window was open! And then he thought— *still* open. How strange—he had quite forgotten it as open: yet this was exactly what he had noticed earlier —in fact what must have suggested what he was about to do—exuberance had driven the thought from his mind, the means ballooning above the end. But here and now was the end . . . he fitted an arrow and aimed.

As he drew the bow a motor backfired out in the streets. The sound crashed into the gardens, sending birds skywards twittering, and for that split of a second all the trees and leaves and walls seemed to shiver and bounce. He loosed the arrow. It went sailing across, but low, as if struck by the sudden convulsion, and whacked like a wasted stick far beneath her window.

His spirits dropped all away from him. The gardens cried out his impotence. The air was all empty. He felt stupid, cursed all the undergraduate absurdity of what

he had been doing—and yet felt a little forlorn, for had
they not played the boy-girl fool together, Lily and he,
finding again a forgotten lightness? But he was alone,
now—he had simply been showing off. It was his old
idiot nature to fabricate some *different* way of doing
things. To act for no good reason on this earth always
obliquely and was this why he had made such a mess
of things in any case . . . ?

He saw himself now too clearly. Seeing is accusing.
Accused, his defences rose. Excuses spilled out—desire
for a window might well end in an arrow, or hell why
not a lassoo or a breeches-buoy, any material communication—and wasn't the arrow a symbol of sex? And
didn't the husband shoot his wife in the thigh as part
of the wedding ceremony somewhere, one of the
Guineas?—and a fury at injustice flashed up hot in him
and another arrow was in the bow and this time gritting
his teeth and wild in anger he shot high in the air, high
at the black whirling cowl on the roof above her window, so high that the shaft twanged far up in a fine
wide arc and then, its exact trajectory found, dived
straight and true at her window and in.

His spirits yelled delight! His arrow was in! He
snatched another into the bow, aimed now at the grin-
ning black mask of the cowl, and shot hard.

At that moment, like an actress on cue, she appeared
framed in the white sashes: peering, his shaft in her
hand.

The knowing arrow curved down like a wing and
struck her in the centre of the head, erected itself for
a second like a monstrous decoration to the hat she

wore, then sagged like a lowered tail as she herself sank out of view to the floor.

Horror whirled round him. The black empty window square shouted. Yet in that flash he remembered her painting with the newspaper like a redskin head-dress—and then through a wide dark echo-chamber he ran yelling from the room, calling Leslie, calling for an ambulance, out of the front door and running hard along the street.

Round the corner men were repairing the pavement. The little planked corridor left was filled with a woman pushing a pram. He ran into the road and round, brought a car to a squealed stop, started a dog barking and running with him. At number twenty-two he was faced with four bell-pushes. No time to read, he rammed the flat of his palm on all four. Bells buzzed all over the house. With his other hand he banged the knocker echoing up and down the street.

All this time she would be alone in her room, bleeding, struck silently, no one knowing.

He knocked and knocked and thought about breaking down the door—too strong—or jumping onto the nearest window-ledge—too far—or running back and getting over the garden wall again—too long, too long —when steps sounded coming up from the basement and then the door opened.

Standing there was a man who must have been the rose-squirter. Matthew never knew, for this man's face had never been seen—but there was no time to tell or answer his stuttered disapproval, he pushed past and ran hard up the stairs.

Another door. No bell, and he slammed on it with his fists and prayed for the first time that Dawn was at home. She was, she had heard her bell rung, and he nearly fell through the door as she swung it open and sharp as a whip snapped: "What the hell's all this?"

But he was in and past her, shouting: "It's Lily— Lily's hurt!" and he had flung open her door to see Lily on her knees, rising, with the arrow in her hand, looking at it dazed, as if it were a long way off.

He fell down on his knees by her and slowly, with infinite care in so much rush, lifted her hat from her head. It was a small curled felt hat, its brim doubled back and trimmed with some kind of cord. It was torn where the arrow had struck. On her forehead beneath, dead white as from loss of blood, no more than a small rose bruise showed, no blood, no hurt.

"I thought I was shot," Lily kept saying, "I passed out." And then, "What *is* this? Where does it come from? Kids? I passed out. . . . "

"Oh thank God," Matthew could only say, over and over again, holding her shoulders as if he wanted to prove to his hands she was there at all.

"What happened? Why are *you* here? I'd like a glass of water," Lily said.

Above them Dawn was standing, a giant figure, powdered military jaw, dark eyebrows frowning, pink hair and a blue housecoat on which swansdown gently blew in the draught from the window. "What *have* you been doing, darling?" she said, like a mother with a bleeding but muddy child, "and what's this type up to?"

"Shut up!" Matthew said. "And get a glass of water."

And Dawn did. Quietly, looking almost feminine in sudden submission.

"Oh God, it was mad, I shot it," Matthew stuttered, stroking her forehead.

"My hat!" Lily shouted. "Oh—my *hat!*" she said angrily as she saw the tear in it. The colour came back to her cheeks.

"Thank heaven for your hat," Matthew whispered.

"*You* shot me?" she said. She might have been asking about some pleasing gift, a bouquet of flowers, for the smile she gave him, the smile of eyes seeing his face now suddenly near, eyes searching about his face with interest, as if looking for pimples.

He said nothing but pointed at the paper round the arrow-head.

"But why?" she laughed unbelief. "Why shoot me? You weren't *that* angry?"

He shook his head and pointed at the note, but she could not understand and so it was he who had to undo the little piece of paper.

He smoothed it out and she took it, reading still puzzled. "Well," she said, "don't we all?"

He looked over and read: "Darling Lily, I love Matthew."

He had forgotten the arrow shaft, there was a hole where the "you" had been

"No, not me—*you*," he muttered, "there's a you there," and he poked his finger at the little hole and it went right through.

She swivelled round and put both arms about his

neck and hugged him. "Oh my dear, that's better, that's *so* much better!" she laughed.

"Better?"

"Better."

He murmured through his lips: "Oh dear how I love you—"

"Here's the water," Dawn said.

Lily looked up still holding Matthew, they were still on their knees like children at a game, dressmakers after pins. "Dawnie? We're going to be married," she said. "Isn't it wonderful?" she shouted.

"Well," Dawn said, "well." And then the look on Lily's face, as faces sometimes shine with delight, broke her, and her mouth opened: "Well good luck," she smiled now hugely, "good luck, my beautiful bulls-eye. He's quite a lad, your boy. They usually get the little tyke with the wings to do it."

She hitched at herself: "And if you don't want a couple of tasty great ambulance men downstairs, I'll take them."

No one answered.

"I guess this is where I came in," she said to the silence and went out.

Matthew was staring at Lily in wonder: "Do you mean it?" he said.

She frowned at him as if he were a child too childish.

"God," he said, "I might have killed you." His stomach suddenly winced as at all images of accidents just averted, crumbling precipices, cars kissing. "I wouldn't have worried," she said vaguely.

"It might have cut straight in . . . " and never in his

life has Matthew quite got over this. The thought of it is like a nail drawn over glass, he has to grit his teeth. No snigger at such a silly game of bow-and-arrows can laugh down that one grave lethal possibility.

When at last they got up, straightening themselves, the tortured moan of tom-cats started from the gardens, two or three old toms must have been squatted staring at each other singing their praises. Lily laughed: "Them too," she said.

And her eye followed the sound out to the gardens and stayed there looking over at his window. He looked too. He was quite surprised to see it empty.

Casually, as if to herself, she said: "I've loved you from the very first moment I saw you."

An awful suspicion seized him. He pointed at his window: "Not—not seeing me over there?"

"No," she smiled. "Not like you. No, when you came here."

"But why then—" he began.

"Why? Why does anyone? I don't know why."

"But—"

"I suppose you fall for something in the look of someone and then you test it getting to know them though you don't really get to know them at all and anyway you passed the test."

"But—"

"What test? *I* don't know. Do you like looking at me when I, what, put a penny in a slot machine?"

"Well—yes."

"Or pick a piece of fluff off my dress or trip on the kerb or anything, *anything*?"

"Of course I do."

"Well you can't say I do these things better than anyone else and you can't say you're thinking of my beautiful mind all the time, so what is it? What do we know about it? Nothing."

He sighed at her. "Can't I get my 'but' in? I agree with all you say—but is it *quite* the moment for a formal diagnosis? What I wanted to—ask is why did you say no what I asked you the other night?"

She looked sly. The tom-cat's moaning rose and fell, gathering force. "Well—your own diagnosis was rather formal at the time, wasn't it?"

"I was only going over what had to be fairly said."

"And you fairly said it, my darling." She shook her head. "No," she said softly. "No, Matthew, a girl wants a proposal not a proposition. Nor an offer of rescue, nor a calculation of the chances of happiness. She wants it all or nothing; all on a plate, please—you know, darling, you might have been waving a profits chart at me—"

"But how could you say *no*," he said.

She smiled slyly. "I couldn't say yes," she said. "Besides, if you really wanted me—you'd come back."

"Then what you said about having fun wasn't—?"

"Oh, those were just things I said. . . ."

And the sly smile grew slyer until it was not sly any more but instead a shocking long look of cunning and wisdom, all innocence seemed to fall from her and not age but ageless duplicity took its place, she looked him straight in the eyes and he found himself staring at a snaky thing, pure knowledge—yet with it compassion and tenderness and pity and no sentiment whatever. For what seemed much longer than the second of time it took, he felt himself in the presence of great and original danger—a second that left him with the slight fear that is called a "hearty respect" for her for the rest of his life. She was a woman. She was capable of anything.

"No, but why . . . " his voice faltered.

"You tell me," she smiled, "you're older."

THIRTEEN

So IN A fine hired morning coat a size too big, full of champagne and filling up with more, cigar and glass and wedding cake in his three hands and a little silver ball from the icing wedged between two teeth like a bright new filling, so Leslie came to the end of his tale —And there you are, he said, waggling his moustaches over to the bride and groom standing black and white by their cake, there you are with a lot of fuss about nothing or, as it might be said, a lot of nothing about life's biggest fuss of all, getting hitched. There they stand, he said, two young people on the brink of a new life—which will begin in a merry little bedroom with a shilling-in-the-meter fire and no shilling, in a hotel with a hundred rooms and real red fire-extinguishers and real servants but no sandwiches after ten, in a heaven-for-two Somewhere in England, where the beer flows like water and the bread is cut into little squares—there they stand and God Bless the Bride, it's Her Day and so help me it does make her look radiant, she's a treat all rosy in the face and a shine in the eyes, feathers in her hair—she's the first I've seen to wear in the hair

white feathers, not flowers, I wonder why. Old Matthew
too, my dear lord-and-m like a naughty big beetle in
his tails, it's good to see the man himself again, and
twice the man, good luck to him. (Though he never
looked half the man, and thereby hangs a moral boys,
if ever you see a man in a suit, sound in limb and the
look of a lord, well-set-up and nowhere to go—reserve
some pity for him, don't spent it all on the well-fed
cripple, there's crippling and crippling here below, the
best-shined shoe's got a hole in the soul.)

Leastways, gentlemen, what's done's done—and here
at heart's ending we have from left to right, all dressed
up and somewhere till 5 p. m. to go our dear Sir Hugh,
who has recorded his speech in his little grey box and
graces the present occasion with long trousers, and
Ligne's old Mum who runs the pisky-store down west
and who's making enough eyes at old Hughie for Les-
the-Wad not to predict a double wedding won't come
of this, and Margot Bondy and her Dr. Bondy who've
brought their little treasure in a carrier-box for all to
see, yes at a wedding too, and over their chatting to an
enchanted Ambassador, a real one and a friend of
Ligne's—why none other than the best-dressed woman
in the room, a cigarette idly dangling from lily-white
fingers, a madly as they say gay bonnet of taupe alfalfa
tilted off one eye, Mrs. Orme.

What else? There's changes back at home. Yours
truly's out and the missus is in and where yours truly's
headed for you'll never guess. Matthew fixed it. Item
One. For the time being—sleeper-in to a nervous dame
who wants a man about the house, doesn't want to see

him, just wants him there, him asleep one side of the house, she on the other, both snoring their backs off with only the walls between—a fitting end to a distinguished Casanova, Loveless Lovelace indeed. And afterwards—Item Two. Down to help Mum with her piskies. *Merchandizing*. Following in master's footsteps. Putting piskies on the map. All the way down to Land's End with a yo-ho-ho and a pint of scrumpy. Makes a change. Thespis—adieu!

But Loveless Lovelace? Who's afoot we've not forgotten? Over by yon gilded basket of blue hydrangeas flush from a morning mannequin-do and due to serve again to-night when Masons meet to dine—who stands teething on a tasty lobster tit-bit and undressing our great big thumping toastmaster with her naughty little peepers but a lady larger than life itself, a blue rinse shadowing her pink for the occasion, my purple-headed beauty, my dear old Dawneroo! Up Guards and at 'em! View hallo! It's every man for himself, me lads, here's meat for the Gods that's no man's poison, so *mind your backs*—and *yours* toastmaster—this is where *I* come in. . . .

And away went Leslie through the wedding swirl to his destined end, Dawn and a free-found bed and piskies, unsinkable flotsam floating one stage further on, away through the wedding guests, this stage of his story done, away through fast-drying tears of bridal sacrifice, through women reminded of their own past Day and all that's happened since, through men at last safe after scared moments top-hatted on the eyeful streets, men now happy to be eating cake and drinking wine at half-three in the afternoon as if they did it every day, as indeed strangely they look used to their fancy formal dress, not at all put out as the story usually goes, through these and all this air of prosperity and the Ascot air of the ladies and the good all-out will of weddings that must centre on the Bride and her Groom, Lily and Matthew, their troubles for the moment over, brilliant in their day, who now stand over the shattered carcass of their cake, above the below-legs life of little bridesmaids dressed as white and fluffy squaws, and who pass to each other now a smile of true understanding, in love and loving it all, the flight, the flurry, the feasting and the fuss.

When they returned from their honeymoon, scoured by the breezes of the south-coast resort they had chosen for just that reason—to make this beginning against a background of chastening reality, rather than in some sub-tropical dream, and to rise above it—they went temporarily to live in Matthew's old house.

It was a happy time. There were plans to be made, the purse-strings were pleasantly open, and what was of course more important was that they had at last the leisure to sit down and find out something about each other. It was during this period that an odd piece of good fortune came Matthew's way. It was not unexpected. But like everything else it had to be experienced to be understood. A simple matter. Dawn moved in to Lily's old room across the gardens.

Since now there were changes in his own house,

Matthew had removed his private study up to the room
that had been Leslie's. And often when Lily was out
and he was alone, the habit of months led him to the
window to look out. All was the same, yet all—as the
advancing weeks of summer erected a new green architecture—different. Now the plane-tree hanging above
Lily's window was lowering real leaves, this was the
last sight of it, in a week the window would be gone.
And as he stood and watched and thought of all the
past weeks, as he allowed himself guiltily, like an addict
of narcotic hours, to re-enter the dream—Dawn's figure
appeared in the window.

For a moment a great fear clutched his heart. For a
moment he felt that everything had been dreamed,
that suddenly he had woken up to the true grey day
with Lily back at her window. For, at that distance,
and shaded a little with the window, Dawn did indeed
look like Lily. The distance and the shadow veiled their
two dissemblances. That figure bowed alone over its
private task might indeed have been his Lily.

Yet—with one extraordinary difference. For Dawn's
greater weight and rougher features, in fact all the
coarseness and the very definition of her came across
the distance to produce for Matthew's disconcerted eye
a wholly curious effect. It was as if a real Lily he could
touch were standing not by his side but there far away
at the window—no more the indistinct woman of his
waking dreams, but a real figure of preposterous definition, tangible as the sill upon which his fingers rested,
destroying all the laws of perspective and reality. And
in this strange way, it was the truth itself he then saw.

He was looking at his dream become magically real. He was experiencing the bubble finally burst and brought, by a moment's chance, immediately to earth, dream become reality in the round.

There was a sound below, a key in the lock, Lily's. The warm feeling came back as he heard it. And he moved away from the window into the house, and went to meet what he most wanted in the world, steps on the stairs.